LANE UNLEASHED

BROTHERHOOD PROTECTORS WORLD

TEAM KOA: ALPHA

BOOK ONE

REGAN BLACK

Twisted Page Press LLC

To Elle, for inviting me into her amazing Brotherhood Protectors World, thank you so much! And hugs all around to Jen, Stacey, Kris, and Lori for making this project such a joy.

BROTHERHOOD PROTECTORS

ORIGINAL SERIES BY ELLE JAMES

Brotherhood Protectors Hawaii World

Team Koa Alpha

Lane Unleashed - Regan Black

Harlan Unleashed - Stacey Wilk

Raider Unleashed - Lori Matthews

Waylen Unleashed - Jen Talty

Kian Unleashed - Kris Norris

Brotherhood Protectors Yellowstone World

Team Wolf

Guarding Harper - - Desiree Holt

Guarding Hannah - Delilah Devlin

Guarding Eris - Reina Torres

Guarding Payton - Jen Talty

Guarding Leah - Regan Black

Team Eagle

Booker's Mission - Kris Norris

Hunter's Mission - Kendall Talbot

Gunn's Mission - Delilah Devlin

Xavier's Mission - Lori Matthews

Wyatt's Mission - Jen Talty

Corbin's Mission - Jen Talty

Tyson's Mission - Delilah Devlin

Knox's Mission - Barb Han

Colton's Mission - Kendall Talbot

Walker's Mission - Kris Norris

Brotherhood Protectors Colorado World

Team Watchdog

Mason's Watch - Jen Talty

Asher's Watch - Leanne Tyler

Cruz's Watch - Stacey Wilk

Kent's Watch- Deanna L. Rowley

Ryder's Watch- Kris Norris

Team Raptor

Darius' Promise - Jen Talty

Simon's Promise - Leanne Tyler

Nash's Promise - Stacey Wilk

Spencer's Promise - Deanna L. Rowley

Logan's Promise - Kris Norris

Team Falco

Fighting for Esme - Jen Talty

Fighting for Charli - Leanne Tyler

Fighting for Tessa - Stacey Wilk

Fighting for Kora - Deanna L. Rowley

Fighting for Fiona - Kris Norris

Athena Project

Beck's Six - Desiree Holt

Victoria's Six - Delilah Devlin

Cygny's Six - Reina Torres

Fay's Six - Jen Talty

Melody's Six - Regan Black

Team Trojan

Defending Sophie - Desiree Holt

Defending Evangeline - Delilah Devlin

Defending Casey - Reina Torres

Defending Sparrow - Jen Talty

Defending Avery - Regan Black

PROLOGUE

*L*ane Benning knew he was running late. He checked his watch and smiled. Barely late. He just couldn't work up any angst about it. The woman he'd been flirting with on the beach was worth whatever grief his pals would dish out. Besides, he was headed to a party that would surely run well into the night. That's what happened when the Navy celebrated one of their own.

Despite his tardiness, he was looking forward to catching up with folks he hadn't seen in a few years, trading stories and memories.

And the barbecue. He could smell it as soon as he got out of the courtesy car that had driven him over from the hotel where he and his four closest friends were staying during this visit.

"There you are." Harlan Fender greeted him with a firm slap on the shoulder. "You're late."

Lane didn't argue, Harlan noticed every damn thing. Made him one incredible operator, but was occasionally annoying in a friend.

The crowd was bigger than Lane expected, gathered in a picnic area framed by potted palms set at regular intervals. Long tables were dressed with flowers and lanterns. If he didn't know better, he'd think this was a party venue instead of a working ranch. Hawaii was incredible. Someone had pulled out all the stops for this setup. A smoker was going on the far side of the field, where the breeze carried the smoke up and away from the guests. Buffet tables loaded with food were anchored by a row of coolers, spilling over with ice and drinks.

On the opposite side of the field, a band started playing, the lilting island beat setting a festive mood.

"Did I miss anything?" Lane asked.

Rick "Raider" Torres, another one of his crew, extended a longneck bottle of beer. "What the hell took you so long? Gadsden's been asking about you."

Lane wasn't so sure about that. He was only fifteen minutes behind the official start time listed on the invite. And the part of him that had relaxed after retiring was a little surprised to see so many people here already.

Four of his closest SEAL teammates—Harlan, Raider, Waylen Brown and Kian Fox—the men he'd ridden with into hell and back with time and again, kept telling him his sudden disregard for clocks was abnormal. Looking around, he thought they might have a point.

Of course, this was a party for their former commanding officer. One of the best, in Lane's mind. Maybe he shouldn't have pushed the envelope by even fifteen minutes. During his years of service Lane and his pals had given Glenn Gadsden their best effort, every time. Gadsden was one of the good guys, known for his unflappable demeanor, his fair and stern approach, and for backing team decisions on field ops even when things went to hell.

Especially when they went to hell.

As a CO, Gadsden had been one hell of a leader, popular up and down the chain of command. He'd never been a micromanager, so it was hard to imagine that he'd be overly concerned with Lane's delayed arrival.

"Well, I'm here now." Lane glanced around. "And ready to party all night."

"Fair point," Raider said.

Behind Harlan, Waylen and Kian approached. "Gang's all here. Finally." Waylen aimed a hard look at Lane. "Surprised you're alone." He liked to pretend he used his superior computer skills to keep tabs on anyone at any time. "What was her name?"

Lane hadn't been graced with that...yet. Ignoring Waylen, he caught Kian's attention. "Did we get him a card or something?" He might not mind the clock well these days but he knew that task hadn't been assigned to him.

"Or something," Raider interjected. "His favorite whiskey."

Lane recalled that debate now. He'd sent Harlan money to cover the gift.

"And we came out to Hawaii for his party," Kian said. "Or have you forgotten where you are?"

No, he hadn't forgotten. From the volcanoes to the jungles to the beaches and fabulous surfing, it was hard to confuse the lush Hawaiian Islands with anywhere else in the world. A little flirting at the resort, then out here for the party equaled the best Saturday night in a while in Lane's estimation.

Waylen studied Lane, his gaze narrowing. "You're working on something."

Raider shook his head as if just being Lane's friend was a trial. "Or someone," he joked. "Lane can always find trouble. You can't claim it's out of character today."

While his four best friends piled on, Lane let their grumbling and speculation roll off. Jokes aside, they were always giving him grief about his timing. In the field his timing had been perfect. And to a man, his SEAL teammates appreciated those efforts. But in the six months since their retirement, he'd earned a reputation for either being too early or too late.

Now that he was done with the military rigor, he

was enjoying running on his own schedule. He'd shown up a day early for the cruise they'd taken to the Bahamas. Being an hour late to dinner was typical. And he'd missed a flight entirely a few months back. All things considered, they should be pleased he was already here.

There were worse bad habits.

If he confessed to being distracted by the beautiful brunette with golden skin and stunning curves highlighted by that tiny sizzling pink bikini, his friends would understand how miraculous it was that he'd shown up at all. But that would mean his friends would've seen her too and that made him edgy. That surge of possessiveness wasn't typical for him. Then again, the woman hadn't been typical.

"There's a guest book and a place to write a personal note for the big scrapbook his wife is pulling together," Kian said.

Harlan elbowed him. "Come on. I'll introduce you to Hawk." He nodded to a small cluster of people chatting near a smoker. Close by, he recognized a traditional pig roasting pit. "That's him. Arm around his wife. Her dad is manning the smoker."

"This is a big operation." Lane looked around, impressed all over again. He understood the concept of 130,000 acres dedicated to this ranch qualified it as immense, but somehow seeing the big party space they'd created struck him a little differently. He couldn't see any livestock. Only the house and one barn.

As they moved through the crowd, he greeted men and women he recognized. He'd traveled the world with many of the people here on various teams and assignments and training exercises. He wondered if it was just him, or if everyone struggled to find their way when they returned to civilian life. It helped to have Harlan, Raider, Waylen, and Kian, but the five of them couldn't travel indefinitely. And he should probably find a hobby beyond flirting at every opportunity.

Jace "Hawk" Hawkins had found his place with a wife and a new purpose right here in paradise. A ranching operation that served as headquarters for a fresh branch of the Brotherhood Protectors, a group originally founded by former SEAL Hank Patterson back in Montana.

"We're not in Montana anymore," Lane murmured.

"What's that?" Harlan asked.

"Nothing."

What would it be like to have a new purpose, to settle down and start a family? He could make a case for settling in Hawaii. Gadsden had the right idea to retire here, among friends he'd made during his last duty station.

Hawaii boasted so many spectacular views and entertainments. It was one of the most incredible places Lane had ever seen. He could see the value in settling down out here. Not like he had anyone out there in the world expecting him to show up—aside from his friends.

An image of the gorgeous brunette popped into his mind. No sense getting hung up on her, she was a tourist passing through, same as Lane.

Harlan introduced Lane to Hawk and his wife, Kalea, gave Lane a warm welcome. "Some place you've got."

Kalea's dad, John Parkman, gave a firm nod. "Thanks. We're glad to have the help and support these days."

Lane had heard the short version of Hawk and the new Brotherhood Protectors out here. The team was just getting started, all of them former military folks who weren't ready to be done with stepping up and doing the right thing when someone needed help. That had been Hank's vision from the start and his commitment to growing regional teams was good news for the area and for the people who joined the effort.

If Hank wanted a team out here it was for a good reason. To an outsider, it might be hard to believe there was that much trouble out here in the middle of the Pacific, but Lane knew better. Trouble was everywhere and covered petty crimes to big criminal operations. Even in paradise, trouble could find a foothold.

There were times when Lane got frustrated at how much people sucked. He shoved away the unpleasant thoughts. No need to brood on such a gorgeous day. He was among friends and, more importantly, among people who understood what it meant to go the distance for the team.

Something Gadsden had emphasized throughout his career with the teams. Something worth celebrating.

The conversation veered back to the guest of honor and as more and more people arrived, everyone traded stories, enjoying the music, food, and company.

About an hour before sunset, as tiki torches were being lit around the picnic area, the first sign of trouble rumbled underfoot. Lane had never been in an earthquake, and this didn't feel at all the way he thought it should.

It was like standing on distant thunder, the sound rolling through him, unsettling and short lived. The band kept playing, but most of the guests stopped talking, looking around at each other as concern mounted.

The next disturbance wasn't as easily ignored. He looked to the south, where the sound was coming from. Kilauea, the most active volcano on this island, had decided to make its presence known. In the fading light Lane could see the rising plume of smoke and ash, highlighted by what must've been the sparks and glow of spewing lava.

A stunned silence fell over the crowd, followed by a rush of everyone talking at once. Phones were aimed toward the southern sky. And the sky delivered an awesome display as the volcano blew in a sudden, glorious rage.

"This wasn't on the schedule," Lane said to the guys around him. "But it's a helluva show for Glenn."

"Don't they usually know about these things?" Harlan asked.

"It's nature," Waylen said. "Don't worry, no one's gonna ask you to talk it down."

"Unpredictable is the norm," Raider said.

"And what do we do?" Lane wondered.

"Hello!" Kalea's voice carried over the party as she stepped to the microphone. "Can I have your attention, please?"

Lane hadn't even noticed the band had stopped playing.

Kalea's father joined her on the stage. "Everyone, please stay calm," John said. "We're not in immediate danger out here."

"Just some extra excitement for Glenn," Kalea said. "When the volcano gets moody, it spouts off at the ocean, usually to the south, well away from us." Nervous laughter moved through the crowd. "That said," she continued, "if you have any breathing issues or concerns, let me know. Any ash, if it does blow this way, might cause some discomfort. It's no problem at all to find you a comfortable place to relax inside."

John and Kalea gave the microphone back to the band.

Across the field, Lane caught sight of Hawk and his team striding away from the gathering. He elbowed Raider, who was also tracking them. "Let's go."

His friends were in immediate agreement, moving out without needing to say a word. None of them would stand by and watch if there was something they could do to help.

"Hey!" Harlan called out as the five of them trailed Hawk and the others. "We can pitch in. Whatever you need."

Hawk turned and seemed to scan all five of them with a single glance. "Good. We could use the extra hands."

Lane had questions about island safety protocols and procedures, but he kept his mouth shut. In the headquarters building, Hawk turned on a monitor and brought up a map of the Big Island. Then he turned up the volume on the emergency radio.

"All right," Hawk said. "I want to spread out as calls come in. You can see the small towns on the perimeter of the island. First responders are few and far between. Roads too." He pointed out the hospitals, a couple of clinics, and the fire stations. Before he could say more, the radio crackled with the first calls for help. Fire. Injury. Smoke and ash.

His jaw set, he took a breath and pointed to the map. "That's all southwest of us. This eruption isn't spewing into the ocean. These towns can get cut off in a hurry. The ash cloud alone can pose serious health problems and choke vehicles."

As calls came in, Hawk assigned a man and sent him off with a radio and a vehicle if necessary. "Stay in contact with us here. We can coordinate more help if you need it. Just do what you can to help folks get out of the danger zone. We'll keep you informed about emergency shelters, if and when they open."

Lane waited, listening and watching, as one by one, Hawk dispatched his team to answer various calls and offer support around the island. Reports of fires and blocked roadways and injuries kept coming in. His pulse slowed as his focus intensified. He had to remember there were local first responders out there, it wasn't up to this modest group of retired SEALs to handle every crisis.

Then a video call came in directly to Hawk's cell phone. He put it on the monitor and the face that appeared on the video shocked Lane almost more than the volcano itself.

It was the brunette from the beach. She wasn't in a bikini now. Instead she wore a shirt with colorful flowers and her hair was pulled back from her face.

"Hawk, I'm in trouble," she said.

"Where are you?" Hawk asked, voice cool and even.

Lane's heart thundered in his chest as he waited for the information.

"The resort. One of the kids under my protection is missing. Possibly kidnapped."

The resort. Where he'd been flirting with her earlier. "Send the info to my phone," Lane declared, grabbing a radio. "Tell her help is on the way." He paused at the door. Swore. "I need a ride."

Hawk tossed him a set of keys. "Plate number is on the tag."

With a nod, Lane ran out into the night that was growing more chaotic by the minute.

1

---

*O*ut on the balcony of the hotel room, Cassie Marner looked to the south. Billowing clouds of ash were rising over a hazy glow from the erupting volcano. The sheer power of it, even from this supposedly safe end of the Big Island, was crazy.

Intimidating. Overwhelming.

She'd never felt so small, which was a serious admission for a farm girl from Iowa with a nose for trouble and a heart for adventure. Her mom would be proud—and probably a little fearful—if she could see Cassie now.

Cassie felt the fear, but she couldn't wallow in it. Couldn't let it drag her off course.

A Guardian Agency protector, she was in charge of personal security for Judith Knowles, her husband David, and their two children Josie and

Dillon. The nanny, Mandy Cox, fell under the protective umbrella as well.

Judith was a civilian employee at the Pentagon, overseeing billions of dollars in contracts in the procurement office. Six months ago, trouble had come knocking. Vague warnings for her to cooperate with shady demands had turned into specific threats against her children.

Judith and David hadn't wasted time. They'd taken their concerns to Gamble and Swann of the Guardian Agency.

Cassie and her partner, Drake Vogel, had been assigned to keep the family safe until the source of the threats could be found and eliminated. The two of them had quickly found a rhythm with a family of genuinely kind people.

The Knowles were the good guys, in Cassie's opinion. Warm, friendly, and hardworking. Integrity in spades. This Hawaiian vacation was a reward after months of stress and uncertainty. As much as the parents had shielded the kids, having bodyguards around clearly emphasized the issue. Still, Josie had finished eighth grade with honors and was all about moving on to high school. Her little brother was a pistol, though his third-grade teacher raved about his reading ability. Cassie hadn't protected kids before and right up until an hour ago, it had been an excellent experience.

Now, she knew if she didn't find Josie and bring her home, she'd never forgive herself.

She dialed Drake's number again, listened to the call go straight to voicemail.

Not a good sign.

Cassie heard the glass door open behind her and braced herself for the inevitable query.

"Has there been any word?" Judith asked. The stress and worry were clear in the puffy eyes and hard lines bracketing her mouth. Her short blond hair—usually perfectly styled—was mussed from her fingers shoving through it.

Cassie checked her phone, a perfunctory exercise, then shook her head. "I'm sorry. No." She'd tried to reach Drake over and over since the zipline tour group had returned without him and Josie.

"They weren't anywhere near the volcano," Judith mused.

"And the zipline tour guide didn't report any injuries," Cassie added with all the patience she could muster. They'd been over this multiple times. Without more information, there wouldn't be any progress. "I've called for assistance," she said. "And additional security."

Judith pushed at her hair again. "You think this is related to the original threats."

Cassie nodded. Her client was no fool. "I need to get out there and look for Josie. I also need to be sure we're not leaving the three of you vulnerable to a secondary attack."

"How did they find us? What could be worse than kidnapping my daughter?"

Cassie refused to give voice to any of the grim options that popped into her mind. Nothing about this felt right. None of it fit. For months they'd been digging for a lead. To have this happen now? There was more going on, even if she couldn't pin down exactly what that might be.

Into the heavy silence, Judith said, "David wants to help you search."

No surprise there. "I'll talk to him."

Judith stepped forward, her voice low. "You won't let him?"

Cassie shook her head. "Best if he stays here with you and Dillon."

"Safety in numbers?"

If only. "Something like that," Cassie replied. She guided Judith back inside where her husband and son were watching cartoons on the television.

"News?" David asked.

"Not yet." Judith managed a smile for Dillon.

"I've called for help from a nearby team managed by a former Navy SEAL," Cassie explained. "I'm not sure who he will send, but hopefully they'll have search and rescue skills," she continued. The volcano would have a big impact on who would be available. "Gamble and Swann are vetting available personnel in the area to maintain your security while I search for Josie." She held up a hand when David started to volunteer.

"You need to stay here," she said firmly.

"I could help you," he insisted. "My baby girl is out there," he added, his gaze haunted.

His words pinched Cassie's heart. "And she's not alone," she reminded him. "Drake is with her." There was a reasonable explanation as to why he didn't answer her calls. Had to be. "In a typical kidnapping, we'd have a ransom demand by now."

Judith and David exchanged a long look. "Should that make us feel better?" David asked.

"Yes," Cassie replied. "Hang on to that. The silence is a positive sign."

"And you've been teaching us self-defense and survival stuff," Dillon piped up. He was now perched on the back of the couch, looking like an inquisitive owl with his glasses sliding down his nose. "Josie's super into it."

Cassie managed not to cringe. The lessons had started on a whim and weren't exactly sanctioned by the parents. "You're right about that."

Judith brightened and tapped her wrist. "She was wearing that survival cord bracelet you gave her."

Cassie hoped the girl wouldn't have to use it. "True." She cleared her throat. "Let's make a plan for when help arrives." She checked her watch.

17

"Should be any minute now. With your approval," she began, "I'll search for Josie and Drake while the three of you wait here. Extra security will be posted in the hall and at the door so no one else can cause you trouble here."

Judith and David had a few questions, but really, there was nothing to do until help arrived. She hoped like hell Hawk sent her someone familiar with the island terrain. Someone who could keep their wits about them.

Well, that description would surely apply to anyone in Hawk's professional acquaintance.

"And when Josie and Drake come back?" David asked. "What then?"

She appreciated his positivity. They needed all the hope they could drum up right now. "At that point, I think it's best to get the four of you back home, assuming we can get you off the island."

"Because of the volcano?" Dillon asked, eyes wide.

She smiled at the boy. "This eruption will make traveling tricky, but you're not in immediate danger."

"Aw man." He scowled. "I wanted to see lava. In person."

"Still could happen, bud," David said. "We'll talk about it once your sister gets back."

Cassie stepped aside to try Drake again. Were

Josie and Drake missing due to the volcano creating havoc during the tour or was there more going on?

Sometimes being the head of a protection detail felt like she was walking a tightrope between proactive security and reactionary paranoia. And the Knowles assignment meant juggling a ton of variables. Good plans didn't mean things always went smoothly. So many little things had been off lately, but nothing this serious.

A dropped call had prevented a timely pickup, making Judith late for one of Josie's volleyball games. Drake and David had shown up at the wrong restaurant for a business meeting. Cassie hadn't worried too much about those incidents. Technical glitches happened to everyone. Then Drake had a flat tire, leaving Dillon stranded at school for nearly two hours.

According to the school receptionist, another father had brought Dillon to the office to wait. But Cassie hadn't been able to track down that father to thank him. The name he'd given had either been bogus or misunderstood.

Cassie had to assume the worst, for the sake of the client. She and Drake had picked apart every aspect of those moments that had gone awry. The Knowles weren't upset, but the Guardian Agency didn't tolerate average effort. They were the best for a reason.

And then Mrs. Knowles started receiving ads for alternate security services.

That pissed off Cassie and she started suspecting the little issues were some kind of sabotage. But no matter how they dug into it, there was no evidence to back up her theory.

Hawaii should've been a break for all of them, a paradise respite from the normal routine and pressures. She and Drake had assumed it would also mean a break from the threats aimed at Judith. Instead, things had suddenly gone from minor mishaps to potential tragedy.

Lousy, unpleasant scenarios kept chasing through her mind, each worse than the last.

The door to the suite opened and Mandy walked in, her face somber. "Just me."

The nanny had been unable to sit still, so Cassie had let her search the resort grounds for any sign of Josie.

The Knowles swarmed Mandy, asking questions. Cassie barely heard the young woman's answers. If Drake and Josie were in the resort, he would've checked in ages ago. Especially once Mandy had come looking for them.

"When I was in the lobby, another group returned from the zipline tour," Mandy was saying. "But Josie wasn't with them."

Cassie whipped around. "What do you mean? The guide said they all came back together."

"I guess not." Mandy's shoulders slumped. "Apparently, the tour got separated at some point."

This was the first Cassie had heard of any separation. Her instincts shifted into high gear and it took all her restraint not to jump down Mandy's throat for the details. "How many people?"

"Three. Two men, one woman. She looked scared." Mandy swiped at a tear on her cheek. "I asked them about Josie and Drake. Showed them pictures. The woman remembers them on the tour, but doesn't know anything about where they might be."

"Did you get her name?" Cassie asked. "A room number?"

Mandy shook her head. "I gave her my phone number and she promised to call if she thought of anything else."

"What about the men?"

"They didn't have anything helpful to add." Mandy frowned. "They were acting really cocky, like it was no big deal getting stuck out there."

"Names? Room numbers?" Cassie prompted again.

"No. But I snapped a picture when they weren't looking." She turned her phone for Cassie to see it.

The quality wasn't perfect, but it was a start. The faces weren't familiar to her, so Cassie sent the image to herself as well as to the office. The

Guardian Agency research team had remarkable skills when it came to things like this.

Cassie was tired of waiting. Everything inside her was clamoring that Josie needed her. Drake needed her. She reached for her phone, ready to call her bosses when the device started ringing. Caller ID showed the name of Claudia with a number out of the Chicago office. Claudia was considered the number one tech and research support at the Guardian Agency. Cassie was glad to have her on this.

"What do you have for me?" she answered.

"Not too much," Claudia replied. "I'm sending you the last known location of Drake's phone. Josie's phone is offline."

Not a surprising status, but Cassie's stomach clenched. "What was her last known position?"

"Resort lobby."

That didn't make any sense.

"I realize that's not adding up," Claudia continued. "I'm working on it."

"All right."

"You're not on speaker?"

"Correct." Cassie moved back out to the balcony anyway, closing the door behind her. "You found something else?"

"That picture you just sent in, from the nanny's phone," Claudia clarified. "One of those men is employed by Welker Specialists."

Cassie did a double take. Welker had a reputation in security circles for an aggressive approach. They rarely took on small operations like the Knowles case, preferring bigger corporate clients. So what was he doing here? Cassie didn't believe the man just happened to be on the same zipline tour as Josie and Drake. Too bad she didn't have any solid intel to connect the dots.

"Name is Steve Greenlee," Claudia said. "He's listed as a driver on their transport team. Has two arrests for burglary in the past three years. Charges were dismissed. He's a creep, although that's just my opinion."

Great. As if she didn't have enough to worry about. "At least he and his pal are here and not out there with Josie."

"Small mercies," Claudia agreed. "I'll keep working on facial recognition for the other two. We have extra security sorted and headed your way. Names and IDs should be in your inbox."

"Thanks."

"Good luck out there," Claudia said. "I'll be tracking you. Call if you need me."

Cassie ended the call and checked the message with names and information for the supplemental security team a moment before someone knocked on the door.

Judith and David surged forward when she answered, ever-hopeful it would be Josie.

The man and woman were dressed like any other tourists at the resort, but Cassie recognized the steel in their serious expressions. After verifying the new arrivals, she invited them in and made introductions.

"Keep the suite and family secure," Cassie directed. "Once we find Josie, the goal is to move the family to another secure location." Preferably a location without any random Welker personnel milling about. "Direct any questions to the Chicago office and any emergencies beyond your scope should go through the local police."

With a nod for Mr. and Mrs. Knowles, Cassie yanked open the door.

And ran smack into a stranger in a blue Hawaiian shirt with a palm leaf design. She pulled the door closed behind her. "Who the hell are you?"

Then she recognized the short blond hair going gray at the temples, the trim beard and those pale blue eyes. Eyes that had been sparkling with mischief when she'd last seen him in board shorts out on the beach. They'd bumped into each other a few times in recent days and the man had flirted with her shamelessly.

"Cassie Marner? I'm Lane Benning." He stuck out his hand.

She ignored it. "Good for you." The man was sexy as sin, but she did not have time for his antics right now. "If you'll excuse me." She edged by him, unwilling to wait another minute to start her search.

"Wait." He hustled after her. "Hawk sent me."

She stopped short. "Hawk. Sent. You." She couldn't believe this.

The man nodded. "I'm here to help. Whatever you need."

"Are you a native? Familiar with the island?"

"Not native." His blue eyes were serious. "You mentioned a kidnapping."

"You're search and rescue trained?"

"Pretty much." He showed her a California driver's license. As if those couldn't be faked.

She studied it. "How do you know Hawk?"

"Military ties."

Cassie waited, but he didn't volunteer more details. "And the last time you rescued a kidnap victim?"

To her shock, he actually seemed to give that some thought. "About eighteen months ago. What's the ransom? You have proof of life, right?"

She shook her head, incredulous. He said all the right words. Maybe she was desperate, but she wanted to believe he could be helpful. "No demands so far," she admitted. "No contact. If Hawk sent you, I guess that's good enough for me. Come on."

rap. Lane felt a rare stab of guilt. Hawk should've sent Harlan to help her. Lane was the guy in the sniper's nest, not the one who did the talking when things went to hell.

A trained hostage negotiator, Harlan could talk rust off a bumper and everyone was happier for it.

Too late now. He'd seen her face and followed his gut. He was here and he would help her. Not like he didn't have skills of his own.

"What's your plan?" he asked as they rode the elevator down to the lobby.

"My plan is to go out there and find the missing girl."

She stopped as the elevator doors parted. The lobby was crowded with anxious people. Lane didn't blame them. The volcano on the other end of the island was a serious threat, in various ways, to everyone.

"I've got a vehicle with me," he said. "On loan from Hawk."

She turned to him. "All terrain?"

"Yeah. An older Jeep Wrangler, stripped down. Sturdy though."

"Perfect." She stretched out an arm. "Lead the way."

"Who is she to you? The missing girl," he clarified as they jogged for the Wrangler.

"She's the oldest daughter of my client. Her name is Josie. She's thirteen and smart as a whip. I know she can be overpowered, but I also know she would've put up a fight. And my partner was with her. He's good. One of the best really. So the disappearance, the lack of contact, doesn't make sense to me."

In Lane's mind all of that intel, given voluntarily, was a good sign that she trusted him at least a little. He hadn't liked her immediate dismissal of him as useless. For the first time in his life, he regretted flirting with a woman.

"Can you tell me who you're protecting?" he asked as they reached the vehicle and loaded up.

"Judith Knowles is the official client. She and her husband and the kids are all here on vacation. My agency has been trying to track down who's been threatening her these past few months."

"No leads?"

"Nothing solid," Cassie admitted. "Believe me, it pisses me off."

"But you're sure she's at risk?"

"Absolutely." She drummed her fingers on her thigh. "Judith isn't a woman who gives into paranoia. Someone is trying to intimidate her and control her decisions."

"But you don't have any ransom demand."

"No, we don't." She shook her head. "As I said, it's not making much sense."

"Where were Josie and your partner headed?"

"The hotel offers zipline and waterfall tours," she replied. "I'd like to get up there to the trailhead and see what we can find."

"Sure thing," Lane said. He knew the general area. "I did one of those the other day. Have you tried it yet?"

"Flying through the trees on a wire isn't my thing."

"It's a safe wire," he interjected. Couldn't help himself. "Bad for business otherwise."

She gave him an arch look that made him want to tease her more. Somehow, he kept his mouth shut.

"Drake, my partner, has more daredevil tendencies than I do."

Except now both he and the girl were gone. Lane was determined to help Cassie through the crisis. "Are you afraid of heights?" He needed to know if they'd be battling her fear on this search in addition to whoever was behind the disappearance.

"Let's say I'm height-averse. It's not such a phobia that it will get in the way."

He glanced over, impressed by the stern set of her shoulders. The woman had an iron will and he respected that. "Hey, I'm sorry about your client. And I'm not judging you about heights or anything else. Everybody's got something that trips them up."

She relaxed enough to give him a half smile. "Oh yeah? What's your Kryptonite?"

"Well." He sucked in a dramatic breath. "*Officially* I am impervious to everything. It's a Navy thing."

"Uh-huh."

"Unofficially," he continued. "If I never saw another spider, I'd be a happy man." He thought he heard her chuckle but it could have just been a rough exhale as he forced the Jeep off the paved road and up into an off-road trail. "So, if your partner is with the girl and you're with me, who's guarding your client?"

"The protection agency I work for sent temporary reinforcements to keep them safe and guide them in case a ransom demand comes in."

"You trust those reinforcements?"

Her shoulders hunched. "I have to. Because I'm the only one I trust to get Drake and Josie back."

The path was clear and well maintained, but the old Wrangler wasn't exactly built for a smooth ride. The canopy of the rainforest towered over them, filtering the evening light so it seemed as if they were driving through a tall green tunnel.

"If you're familiar with this tour, can you think of any place they might have been ambushed?" she asked.

"Throw a dart," he said. "Most of the trails are narrow between the zipline platforms. And if you have been in Hawaii more than five minutes, you know the jungle is happy to keep its secrets."

"But they were out here with a tour group," she pressed. "How is it possible that no one noticed an ambush or an attack? Why didn't they realize people were missing?"

"You'll see," he said. Experience was really the only way to make her understand how a kidnapper might've created a way to grab the girl and her bodyguard.

"The guide told me he did a head count at every point," she added. "I guess he could've been lying."

Most likely. Lane kept the thought to himself. It wouldn't give her any comfort. Besides, he knew from experience that a crack team could turn many "impossible" plans into reality.

"We'll find the answers you need. If the guide kept counting, then whoever did this was smart enough to keep the same number of people moving along the trail."

"That's disconcerting," she said after a minute.

"More than a little," Lane agreed. "But that means we should find clues."

She was silent for what remained of the drive to the head of the trail. "I can push the Wrangler further but we'll probably have better luck picking up a trail on foot."

"Is that your expertise? Picking up trails?"

"Just one of many skills that might come in handy," he said with pride.

They got out of the vehicle, and he was impressed when she checked two handguns, a twenty-two at her ankle and a Glock 19 at her hip.

"Am I supposed to assume you were a Navy SEAL?" She pulled a flashlight from a pocket on her thigh and turned it on and off again before dropping it back inside. "I know Hawk is a former SEAL, so it stands to reason. I guess."

She doubted him. Big time. "Is there a reason you're struggling to believe I could've served on the teams?"

Her nose wrinkled. "I don't mean to offend. It's just… Where are the usual tattoos? For starters."

"Maybe you just don't know me well enough yet to get to see them."

A smile flickered across her face. "The compass on your shoulder is impressive."

"Nice of you to notice." That was his only tattoo. The meaning behind his ink encompassed far more than he wanted to explain right now. Would've been a better ego boost if she'd mentioned her awe of his shoulders, but that wasn't why they were out here.

He unlocked the gear kit in the back of the Jeep, pleased to find emergency flares and water in addition to a SIG Sauer nine-millimeter, ammunition, and a knife. He loaded up quickly, grateful for the familiar tools he'd used during his career.

"Tell me about the girl."

"Thirteen, as I said. Blonde, five feet tall and slim, almost skinny," Cassie said. "She's athletic. Plays on the volleyball team and runs track too."

Good fitness was a positive. "Any survival skills?"

"Yes." Cassie perked up. "I've been coaching her a bit on self-defense and situational awareness. She isn't ready for any kind of military field test, but she's no dummy."

"Only your partner was armed, right?" He braced for an irritable reaction to what could be considered an absurd query. He had to ask. Having the right intel made a difference.

Cassie nodded absently. Her gaze was on the path beyond the meeting area. "How are you going to pick up her trail with so many people coming and going up here?"

He understood that to the average person the

task seemed daunting, possibly outlandish. But this was his wheelhouse. Now that they were here, Lane was more confident than ever that he was the right man for this job. On the SEAL teams he'd often been the scout, making sure the path was clear for the safety of everyone involved on a mission.

How much of that should he share? He didn't want to brag—then again, he couldn't have her doubting his ability.

"First things first. Let's hike in. We've got to find where they were taken."

Another nod, resolute. "Lead the way."

He started up the path, toward the start of the zipline course. It was immediately clear that a tour guide would be beneficial even though the path was marked with signs. Hawaii was a massive and active wilderness. Everything seemed to be growing constantly. Trees, waterways feeding the ground and sculpting rock, the lava well below them and the evidence of previous eruptions... All of that, along with animals, birds, and the ever present threat of rain? A trail could be erased quickly.

Behind him, Cassie's footsteps were quiet on the path, her breath even. If he didn't know better he'd say she wasn't stressed at all.

"Do you think Josie was taken by someone on the tour?" he asked.

"It just about has to be someone who was out here with them," Cassie said. "The research team that supports me is vetting the other folks on the tour."

Hearing a hitch in her breathing, he stopped short and she nearly plowed into him.

"What is it?" She glared at the surrounding area.

He was focused on her. "You thought of something."

"Yes, I did," she said. "But it's no reason to stop moving."

"Tell me."

Her chin came up and her gaze turned cold as she stared him down. "Who's in charge here?" she demanded. "We're out here to find my client—a child—and my partner. Everything else can wait."

He didn't move. "If you know who did it or have any suspicions, it could help us figure out where they abducted Josie and your partner. Could even shed light on where they took them."

She fanned away an insect. "I don't *know*," she said. "I barely have a suspect. Our best bet is to go into this cold, eyes wide open to any possibilities. Any preconceived notions could mean overlooking an important clue."

"I respectfully disagree," Lane said. "Information is power." Her jaw was set and they were wasting the last minutes of daylight. For now, he'd let her hold on to that power.

Having been on this course with the hotel guide,

he did have an idea of where someone might get separated from the group. In this kind of terrain, it wouldn't be hard at all. Even in broad daylight it was a challenge to see anything beyond more of the greenery and shadows within a few feet off the cleared trail.

She was right to be concerned. With night falling, their search didn't stand much of a chance, but it was clear Cassie wouldn't wait until dawn. He didn't fault her for that. No, he admired her dedication.

"Did you ever serve in the military?" he asked.

"Why didn't you ask me that kind of question out on the beach?"

He laughed. "Cut me some slack. On the beach you were wearing a bikini."

"And you just wanted to get me out of it."

"If you expect me to be sorry for that, I'll disappoint you all day long. If you'd given me your number, we would have had a really nice conversation. Maybe even deep and life-changing." He ignored the scoffing sound she made. "Who knows, your previous career interests could have come up."

Her burst of bitter laughter wasn't flattering. She probably had a point.

Maybe if he tried to be more sincere and open, she would too. Lane had learned early that it was better to own both his faults and his successes. "I know it's obvious that I enjoy flirting," he began. "And blue is my favorite color."

"You flirted with me because my bikini was blue?"

"Call it a level one attraction. Your pink bikini is equally stunning." For a moment, he simply enjoyed the memory. "I talked to you because you're gorgeous, no matter what you're wearing." Did she catch the compliment he was giving her? If so, she refused to engage. "I had high hopes that we'd have drinks or even go out on a date."

"Right."

"You have looked in a mirror recently?" How could she not know she was beautiful?

"That's not what I meant. I'm here on a job."

He waited, but she didn't elaborate further. "I'm all for willing, healthy people hooking up," he said into the silence. "And yeah, my buddies give me crap, but none of them have settled down either."

"Would those be your SEAL buddies?"

"The same," he confirmed. "The five of us came out here for a retirement party over at the ranch where Hawk works."

"And how long are you staying?"

"No idea. The volcano interrupted the party, and possibly altered our timeline." He heard a noise and paused, but nothing came of it, so he pressed on. "I take it your clients don't live in the resort."

"No, they're here on a family vacation. They

didn't advertise the specifics of the trip, not even among their friends."

"Was that your idea?

"It was. We didn't make it a secret by any means or insist that their phones stayed off. But I felt like we had control of the situation."

"Famous last words, right?" He wasn't criticizing her. Operations never went as smoothly as planned. "Every time we were assured we had sufficient intel, I'd want to laugh. There's no such thing."

"I get it," she said quietly. "A gaffe like this is a first for me. Though my assignments have been on a much smaller scale than yours must've been."

He didn't bother acknowledging that. An operation had to be important to those working it. People mattered, lives saved could make a difference. At least that had been his approach whether or not he understood the full scope of the stakes.

"So people knew the family was coming to Hawaii," he said, trying to get back to the matter at hand.

"Yes," she agreed. "We didn't volunteer specifics of which island or which resort. Granted, it wouldn't be hard to find out."

"But you haven't been worried about personal injury or kidnapping until now?"

"Judith was getting threats. Her children were an obvious pressure point so we took precautions."

Lane was grateful that this zipline course was

fairly basic. Sure, the zip lines went through the trees and crossed waterfalls at two places, but in general the hike from one spot to the next was manageable.

"The last pictures I have from Josie show the fourth marker," Cassie said.

"That's not quite halfway," Lane mused, studying the sides of the trail for anything out of the ordinary.

"You either have a great memory or you're just blowing smoke." Cassie said.

"I don't blow smoke. Never saw the point."

"Good to know."

He hoped so. He didn't take that as acceptance or even belief. Only time and results would prove that he *was* an asset to her. He couldn't take her frustration personally. As a professional bodyguard, it was her job to be wary.

Lane searched cautiously around the base of each platform, looking for any indications of trouble before they moved on to the next. He was aware of Cassie the whole time. Her breath, her footsteps, and the general electricity between them.

At the fifth platform, his flashlight caught on a bright yellow wedge of color just a few feet into the forest. "Here we go."

Cassie pressed in close to his side. "Is that a helmet?"

"Yes. Stay back." Lane inched forward, mindful

of his footing. Not everything was as solid as it appeared. When he reached the helmet, that was all he found. No body or belongings. Uneasy, he picked it up and read the name on the tape. "This was Josie's," he called out. He climbed back up to the path, handing it over for Cassie to see.

She swore. Taking a closer look, she noted the busted chin strap.

"I saw that." He hesitated. "When I was out here the equipment was all in perfect working order. I'd say she fought back or it was torn off."

"I don't see any signs of blood," she said.

"That's good." He returned to his search for a trail. It seemed as if the girl had been plucked right out of the tour. "Any chance your man's in on it?"

Her reply was immediate. "Absolutely not."

"All right." He held up his hands in surrender. "That's good."

"You don't believe me?" Cassie demanded.

He spared her a glance over his shoulder. "I believe you," he assured her. "I asked a question, you answered. That's all I need."

She was quiet as they continued along the route. "Why did you ask the question?"

Now they were getting somewhere. "Because if your partner is half as good as you, he wouldn't have let her go without a fight."

"But you don't see signs of a fight," Cassie observed. Her flashlight swept across the area.

"It's dark enough that the scene is hard to read," he admitted. "I'm still looking." He wouldn't quit until she called it. He was sure they were both hoping to find a second helmet. His instincts were firing and he was pretty sure she was expecting the worst.

"So what's between you and Drake?" Might as well make the most of his time with her. If she was involved with someone, he could stop hoping to take her out. After they found the girl.

"What do you mean?"

"Are you partners off the job as well?"

"No."

Good news. Although he wouldn't get ahead of himself just yet. "Is there a significant other in your life?"

She stopped. "Are you seriously asking me this right now?"

"Something else you'd rather discuss?" He plowed on when she didn't react. "When you were out on the beach there didn't seem to be anyone else around who behaved as though they were close to you. Personally, that is."

"No. I'm not involved with anyone," she grumbled. "Even in personal protection, we get some time to ourselves."

They didn't talk further, as they continued to search the path. She wasn't wrong about the challenge. With so many people coming and going regularly with tours, there was no way to discern any activity on the path itself.

Hearing another noise, he paused. Behind him, Cassie froze. His light caught on crushed leaves and a fresh slide of mud that stood out against the thick green forest pressing in. Finally, there was something he could work with.

Cassie pushed past him before he could warn her to wait.

"Drake!" she called. "Josie!"

He heard her swear. And was following her into the forest when she swiveled around to face him. "It's Drake!" She rushed down the slope, sliding to her stop on her knees near the man crumpled on the forest floor.

If she hadn't been so adamant about their partnership being purely professional, Lane would've believed she was in love with the guy.

Battered and bloody, Drake looked as if he'd been hit by a truck. She asked him questions, but so far, he'd only groaned incoherently. While Cassie tried to rouse her partner, Lane searched for signs of the girl. Finding little to go on, he dialed Waylen.

His friend picked up on the second ring. "How's life at the resort with your bikini babe?"

"A little uglier than it should be," Lane replied. "Can you track my phone to see my location?"

"Always."

Lane couldn't be irritated with the confidence. It

41

was exactly the expertise he needed right now. "Good. I'm dropping a pin. We're not too far from the resort. We need someone out here to help transport a wounded man to the closest hospital."

Waylen's voice turned serious. "How wounded? And who is it?"

"Cassie's partner." Lane studied the pair as they spoke in low voices. "Looks like he was beaten up and left for dead. No sign of the kid he was protecting."

Waylen swore.

"My thoughts exactly."

"So there really is a kidnapping?"

"Looking that way. Are you able to get over here or not?"

"Yeah. On my way," Waylen confirmed. "Want me to bring Fox?"

"Couldn't hurt. If he's available," Lane agreed. He had no idea where Hawk had sent his friends. He'd seen Cassie's face and known exactly where he was needed.

"He is. We both are. Hawk has the two of us on standby right now. We'll be there…" His voice went quiet. "GPS says we can get to you within twenty minutes. Assuming it's correct."

"Thanks, man." Lane was forever grateful to his friends. "The two of us will push on to find the kid," he added, keeping his voice low.

Cassie heard him anyway, giving him a subtle

nod. At least she wasn't glaring daggers at him right now. Even in the dim light, he could read the relief in her body language. She was worried, but he suspected hope and determination were on the rise.

"Good luck with that." Waylen cleared his throat. "If you need support, call. Tell your man there to hang tight."

Lane crouched next to Drake and Cassie. "My friends are on the way," he said. "Waylen and Kian. Waylen loves fishing like nothing else and Kian is one of the best medics I know. They know where you are." Lane tucked a bottle of the water into Drake's hands. "Do you have a weapon?"

"Not that I can find," Drake said, his voice thin and rasping. "They're not coming back. Got what they came for." His eyes were swollen, but tears leaked from the corner. "I'm sorry, Cass."

"We'll find her," Cassie vowed. "Take my back-up." She pulled the twenty-two from her ankle holster and handed it to her partner. "I'll let Claudia know what's going on." She gripped his hand. "Hang tough, Drake. You can count on Lane's friends to be here soon."

Her declaration of confidence was surprising. Maybe she was just trying to keep her partner hopeful.

As they moved on, Lane felt guilty leaving Drake behind. Which meant Cassie must be feeling even worse. "My guys will help him. They'll be on site soon." Reminding himself or her? Probably best not to analyze that too closely.

"I know. We have to find Josie."

She sounded one hundred percent focused on the task ahead of them. Not that he could blame her. Innocent kids getting caught up in violence was the worst, in his opinion.

Whatever was going on, the first step was finding the girl and reuniting her with her family as soon as possible.

After that, maybe Cassie would let him take her out for a drink to celebrate.

3

$\mathcal{C}$assie was grateful they'd found Drake alive, and she wished like hell she could stick close and make sure he got to a hospital. But that wasn't the job. She had to delegate and commit all her energy to finding Josie.

She wasn't sure how to correlate Drake's beating with Josie's disappearance. Would the kidnappers be violent with the girl as well? She hoped they had more common sense than to abuse a kid. Terrorizing her with this kind of stunt was bad enough, but actually laying hands on a kid... That was unforgivable.

"We have to find the trail," she muttered. "They didn't just fly out of here." Although she looked up into the dark sky, considering a helicopter escape.

"Anyone mention helicopters?"

"No." Drake hadn't been able to provide much

direction, due to the beating. She stopped short and pulled out her phone.

"What is it?"

"Mandy took a picture. The nanny," she added, anticipating Lane's question. "She was searching the resort for Josie and heard about three people—adults—who supposedly got separated from the tour." She brought up the image on her phone and enlarged it. "There." She held out her phone to Lane. "Do those hands look scraped up to you?"

Lane squinted at the image. "Hard to say for sure. It's possible."

She grabbed the phone back and fired off a text to Claudia. "My tech support says the guy with potentially banged up hands is with Welker Specialists."

Lane didn't react. She backed up a step, suddenly worried she'd miscalculated. Again. What was it about this assignment that she kept making mistakes? She hesitated as he started forward, debating the best way to create some distance from this stranger and make her escape.

"You haven't heard of them?"

"Doesn't ring a bell." His tone was casual, but his gaze was intent. On her, not the path.

She inched backward. The soft ground slid out from under her heel and she started to tumble backward, only to be caught in a vise-like grip. The jerk on her shoulder stole her breath, and the sudden slam into the ground didn't help.

She was stunned, too weak to fight Lane's strong arms as he rolled her away from whatever slope she'd been about to go down. His body surrounded her. His muscles were hard, his breath heaving.

Hard not to be jealous of that while she could barely drag in enough oxygen to stay conscious. Stars danced across her vision. "Let me go," she gasped.

"Sure." He held tightly. "Give me a second." He still didn't move.

"Can't. Breathe." Her heart pounded in her ears.

"Try," he snapped. "You just stripped a decade off my life."

He sounded so annoyed she might've laughed. If she could breathe. And if he hadn't just become a suspect. She felt every ripple as his muscles bunched and shifted beneath her. The heat of his body radiated into hers, chasing away the chill, and sending a warm sizzle through her bloodstream. Dumb move to get all hot and bothered over a man who could very well be her enemy.

She let him ease her upright until they were facing each other, his thigh hot against hers. He found his flashlight and held it so it cast a circle of light over the two of them. He was glaring at her. "What the hell was that? I want that decade, damn you. I have plans for it now that I'm done with the Navy."

His mini-rant left her with more questions and several regrets. "Sorry?"

"Do better." He took a drink from the water bottle and handed it to her.

She drank in small sips until she started to feel better. "I apologize."

"You asked about search and rescue skills," he said, glowering at her. "I know plenty. Starting with suspending a search when the risks are too great."

"We can't stop." The sudden protest sent her into a coughing fit. "Josie needs us," she insisted through her wheezing.

Lane scrubbed at his face, swearing under his breath. "I know you must feel responsible—"

"I *am* responsible."

"Not Drake?"

"Well, he was on the scene, sure, but I'm the lead for the family."

"Buck stops with you."

"That's right," she confirmed, though it hadn't been a question.

"Cassie, we do not have a trail." He closed his eyes as if searching for patience. "Stumbling around in the dark, getting ourselves killed won't help the girl." He shook his head when she started to argue and cast the beam of his flashlight toward the place where she'd slipped. "You were that close to compounding the tragedy out here."

He sounded as if he really cared. About her. She shook off the ridiculous thought. They'd just met—at least as professionals. "You'd find someone else to flirt with," she muttered. "Why don't you know what Welker is?" she asked, pushing to her feet.

"Why don't you know when it's time to suspend a search?" he shot back. "I'm here to help you."

Her fear of him suddenly seemed more absurd than the notion that he cared. He was right and she knew it, even if she couldn't give up.

"Okay. Okay." She blew her hair away from her face. Hauling herself back up to the safer terrain of the path, she sat down. On her phone, she found the link to the tour and studied the map. "Help me talk this through. They attacked back there, leaving Drake for dead."

"Agreed." Lane plopped down beside her, leaning in close so he could see the map too.

His scent wound around her, distracting her. This was so *not* the time and definitely not the man to get mushy over. She preferred the stoic type. Men who exuded an equal measure of character to match any ego and swagger. She wasn't against flirting, she just didn't trust fluffy compliments over real substance.

And that's worked out so well.

She told the pesky voice in her head to pipe

down. They weren't out here to solve her love life, they were here to find Josie.

"I don't know how they got her away from the tour, but there has to be some way out."

"Away from the trails?" Lane shook his head. "We didn't see any signs of that. Your partner is a more likely suspect than I am."

She gaped at him, shocked that he'd read her so well. "What?"

"Don't play dumb." He bumped her shoulder gently with his. "Just get over it. Fast. I'm on your side." He pointed to the map. "With helmets and harnesses and the group spread out enough, the kidnappers could've taken Drake and Josie and inserted two other people while they escaped with her."

He painted a plausible picture. "Still doesn't give us a direction."

"Look at the map." He pointed at her phone. "We missed this service road."

Cassie shivered at the darkness pressing in on them from all sides. "Do we go back?"

He motioned for her to hand him the phone. After a few minutes of scowling, he perked up. "I don't think we need to backtrack. Based on where we found Drake, my money is on them heading this way." He pointed at the map. "This would be the easiest way out of the valley and back to civilization."

That was no comfort at all to Cassie. "And from there, they could take her anywhere."

"One problem at a time." Lane gracefully rolled to his feet and extended his hand. "Once we find the road, we're more likely to see evidence that will guide us to Josie."

Cassie stared up at Lane, far more impressed with him than she wanted to be right now. He led the way as they jogged down the cleared tourist path. At the next zipline platform, he found the access route immediately. The path wasn't as carefully maintained, but they had room to move single file without fighting the thick vegetation.

When they reached the service road, he carefully examined the area, even taking a few pictures of tire treads.

"If you send those to me, I'll have the research team get to work." When the photos came through by text, she forwarded them to Claudia, along with a brief status update.

When she looked up Lane was moving away, his flashlight sweeping back and forth.

She caught up with him and didn't bother asking about a trail. It was clear he was following something.

"Fresh tire tracks," he explained, picking up the pace. "You taught Josie self-defense skills?"

"Yes. Some." She should've been more consistent about it.

"How much do you think she'd remember in a crisis?"

Lane was only asking what Cassie had been wondering since Josie disappeared. "All of it," she stated, utterly confident. "I'm just not sure she'd remember in time to apply the tactics." The admission cost her. Maybe if she'd been more proactive and diligent about the self-defense practice Josie would be with her family right now.

Suddenly her phone vibrated with an incoming message. "It's a text." She paused. "Not Claudia. I don't know this number."

Lane was at her side in an instant. "Ransom?"

Please, no. And yet, if it was a ransom, they would presumably have more information. Braced for the worst, she tapped the screen to see the message. A picture popped up. It was Drake on the ground, much like they'd found him, but the sunlight indicated the photo was taken hours ago. On his chest was a poorly printed photo of Cassie with a red circle and slash over her face.

"That's from this afternoon," Lane said. "Both you and your partner."

She agreed about Drake. "How can you be sure about me?"

"The bikini," he said. "Yesterday's was blue. Today you wore pink."

"Huh." Was it flattering that he had such an excellent recall of her swimwear? "I wasn't on the beach for long," she mused. "If this was taken today, they worked fast."

"Looks like you're the real target," Lane said.

She snorted. "No way. They didn't grab me, they grabbed Josie."

He shrugged a shoulder. "You're out here, separated from your partner, focused on a search instead of your original assignment." He glanced around. "Would you have come out here alone?"

"Yes," she admitted.

"Giving them ample opportunity to take you out."

A shiver rattled down her spine. "I don't care for your theory." Josie's phone had pinged once back at the hotel lobby. By accident or design? What if he was right and Cassie had been deliberately lured away? She swore.

"Because I'm right or...?"

"No one has attacked me yet. Not directly." But this could be another attempt to make her look bad. "Someone—my money is on Welker Specialists—has been messing with us for months."

"How so?"

She explained the incidents she and Drake had overcome while they continued down the road. It didn't take long and going through the list, she wondered if she was just making excuses. Lane frowned as he listened. She wouldn't blame him if he chalked it all up to coincidence. "Forget it. Forget I said anything."

"Not a chance." He looked up at the sky, currently blocked by the trees, then turned his gaze southward. "Who gains if you're out of the way?"

"Me personally? No idea," she replied. "It's irrelevant. We're jumping at any available conclusion when we need to find Josie."

"Hang on." Lane's palm on her arm brought her to an immediate stop. "I'm serious. Could Drake be gunning for your job? Some men don't like taking orders from women."

She shook her head. "No way. That's not how Drake is. Besides, you saw how they left him. He might've died out here if we hadn't found him."

That single shoulder hitched up and down once more. "I've seen people endure worse to avoid suspicion."

She wanted to simply be angry over the implication and couldn't deny there was some logic in what he said. Still, it was an unpleasant thought. Not just the idea of willingly taking a beating, but that Lane had seen worse. Clearly, he'd survived those dark times and he didn't need her pity.

"Not Drake," she repeated. "We both work for the best personal protection agency around."

Lane's eyebrows flexed. "You work for the Brotherhood Protectors?"

She rolled her eyes. "No. I'm with the Guardian

Agency. Let's call it a tie between your group and mine."

"Fine. Does your agency have enemies?"

"Of course." She was sure of it. It was a common enough occurrence in security or any other industry. Whoever sat at the top of the heap had to deal with competitors plotting to knock them out of the way. "Let's table this until Josie is back with her family."

"What if she's bait? I'm serious, Cassie. This could be an elaborate trap to get you out of the way."

Her stomach cramped at the possibility of her charge being used against her. When she trusted her voice, she replied, "Then let's pick up the pace."

Lane caught her once more. "I'll lead."

"Why? Because of your stellar scouting skills?"

"Doesn't hurt," he said, grinning.

A flutter rippled through her, almost as unsettling as the volcano-induced tremors that continued to roll under her feet periodically.

Damn it all, why couldn't she ignore that sexy tilt of his mouth? Or the way he loped ahead with an admirable, confident grace despite the conditions?

"Here we go," Lane said, slowing down as they came to a tight bend in the road. "A vehicle took a hard skid. Surprised it didn't roll," he mused as he examined the area. "Oh. They did. Had to work to get it upright again."

She watched him assess the scene, staying out of his way and listening for anyone or anything that shouldn't be out here. For her, Hawaii wasn't a peaceful refuge. Not because of the work, she loved her job. But the environment was a steady symphony of noise, some soothing, others less so. The ocean crashing into sand and rock, the breezes and rainshowers on the beach, pushing through the trees. And now the volcano on the other end of the island was a source of consistent ambient noise. Since they'd been out here, sirens had drifted their way, along with the acrid scent of sulfur from the ash cloud.

"Over here, Cassie!"

She rushed forward, swallowing hard. "Zip ties."

"Broken zip ties," he clarified. "Did you teach her that?"

Cassie nodded. "Both kids thought they were so cool when they learned how to get free."

His mouth kicked up in a half smile. "She got away," Lane said. "Impressive stuff."

"Wait until you meet her." Cassie had to think positively. She *would* see Josie again and she'd see the Knowles family reunited. Cassie walked the curve of the road, back and forth, then stared out into the layers of dark wilderness beyond the road. "Her phone made it back to the resort with the crew that took her. Those bastards."

"What?" Lane focused on her again. "You mean that photo the nanny took?"

"The same," Cassie confirmed. "Those three have to be involved." She thought about the intel and the warning Claudia had provided. "They took her phone or she left it behind. Either way, Claudia said it pinged at the resort once before it was turned off. It must've been in the vehicle. It's the only scenario that fits."

Lane grunted. In agreement or doubt, she wasn't sure. Didn't care. She was right about this. "Seems strange that a kid could escape three able-bodied adults who needed her for leverage," he said.

Yeah, that bothered her too. In the photo, the three people Mandy had seen didn't appear upset about being left behind. "It explains the lack of demands."

"Does it?" He planted his hands on his hips. "Kidnapping and blackmail are usually about money. Three people beat up your partner and take the girl, only to not give a damn when they lose her?" He shook his head. "This isn't adding up. That photo was a threat against you, not the girl."

Cassie chewed on her lip. If she'd received that picture out of the blue, she would've believed Drake was dead. "We have to find Josie."

"Agreed. And then we'll make arrangements for *your* safety."

She wasn't sure she agreed with him about the last part, but it didn't matter. Once they found Josie and got back to the resort, she wouldn't need Lane to stick around any longer.

Why did that fill her belly with a weird fear of missing out?

4

*L*ane found what might be a trail from the overturned vehicle and carefully followed it away from the service road. Cassie trailed after him, her flashlight poking into the darkness as she called Josie's name.

He wanted to shush her, if only because the person who'd sent that picture might be out here, waiting for the right moment. Whoever wanted Cassie out of the way could be lining up a shot this very second. Lane let the chill slither down his spine. He'd learned not to fight the sensation, but to give his peripheral awareness and his instincts free rein.

It wasn't as if she'd stop calling even if he did ask. She was desperate to find the girl. He understood that. Hell, he was on board with her persistence, he just didn't want her to wind up like her partner. Or worse.

He wondered if the way she'd denied the threat to herself was a common theme in her life. She didn't strike him as a woman with a martyr complex. Then again, he didn't know her. Attraction wasn't the same as connection—something he'd avoided during his years of service.

Through the years, he'd watched relationships crash and burn as forced distance and fallout from various missions took their toll. It wasn't inevitable, but it happened frequently enough that Lane avoided relationships. Why take the chance? After all, if he did fall in love, he'd want the woman he loved to be happy. He would want to be happy too. Military service—especially among the high-pressure SEAL teams—could be a wrecking ball, trashing healthy boundaries and expectations for everyone involved.

"You're quiet," Cassie said.

"You want me to start shouting? She knows your voice, not mine."

"Fair point." She called out again, pausing to listen for any reply.

After a beat, Lane moved forward again. "Why isn't there anyone waiting for you? Besides the client," he clarified. Grateful as he was that he might have a chance here, he couldn't fathom her single. On the one hand, he didn't need to block the way she felt when he'd kept her from tumbling earlier. Her body had felt exactly right in his arms.

The soft weight and warmth of her had sent his imagination into overdrive. He wanted to hold her again, preferably without a near medical crisis in the mix.

"Just not a priority, I guess."

"Huh." Spending time with interesting people was a new high-priority for him. Whether that interest was simple curiosity or more intimate didn't matter. He'd found it was fun to meet people now that he wasn't operating anymore. "Priorities were why you weren't into it when I was flirting with you on the beach?"

"Did I hurt your pride?" She snorted. "Forgive me. I was cool because you're an obvious flirt. Men like you are here one second and gone the next."

Not true. He was in control of his schedule these days. Sure, he traveled with his friends, but he could extend a stay or move on early if the mood struck. Having discovered the benefits of retirement, he was just getting started with living it up.

"And I'm here on a job," she said. "As the lead it feels like I'm on duty twenty-four-seven. My personal hours are a chance to veg out."

He understood the demand and drain of that constant state of readiness. "Right." Maybe he should drop it. But he just pressed for more information. "Am I not your type?"

She tripped and he automatically reached out to steady her. He liked helping her, being close enough to lend a hand. Or anything else she might need or want. "I'd really like to get to know you better."

"And I'd really like to focus on why we're out here. Josie needs us."

He let it go. Mostly because he couldn't figure out why it mattered so much. He flirted all the time, with willing women of course. In the past, if someone wasn't interested, he moved on. Not this time.

Something about Cassie made him want to stick around and win her over. The best chance of earning that opportunity was to find the girl.

Picking his way through the dark, he tried to think like a frightened young teenager running on adrenaline. What would she do, stranded out here without a phone? Did the girl have any sense of direction to go with her basic self-defense skills?

He was about to ask Cassie when his cell phone hummed in his pocket. He stopped, Cassie on his heels. "It's Waylen," he said when the caller ID showed on the screen. "Give me a second."

She nodded, clearly understanding he didn't want to miss a possible clue.

"Tell me some good news," Lane answered. "You're on speaker." He tapped the button and held the phone so Cassie could hear.

"Kian and I found Drake Vogel," Waylen reported. "We're en route to the ER now."

"Thank you," Cassie said.

She smiled at Lane and he was momentarily speechless. "Hey. Yeah. Did you find anything with him?"

"Like what?" Waylen asked.

"A note or something," Lane explained. He was about to elaborate, but Cassie shook her head.

"We didn't look," Fox said. "The man needed medical attention."

"Cassie?" Drake's voice didn't sound any stronger. "Have you found her?"

"Not yet," Cassie said. "We're close."

Lane cocked an eyebrow at the exaggeration and she wrinkled her nose. "You rest up," she said to her partner. "I'll fill you in as soon as Josie's back where she belongs."

There was some muttering in the background, then the sound of an engine. "Keep us in the loop, Benning," Waylen said. "Hawk too. The volcano has everyone scrambling."

"I'll see you soon," Lane promised. "First round is on me." It was a phrase that held double-meaning. There had been times when he'd been responsible for the first—and only—shot on a mission. With that phrase, his friends would understand that he had things under control out here. At least as much as that was possible.

"Hold him to that," Kian said.

The call ended abruptly and Lane slipped the

phone back into his pocket. "I don't renege," he said to Cassie. "He just likes to harass me."

"No worries," she said. "Come on."

She gestured for him to get back to the search. He turned away, looking for clues. She gave another shout, but there was no answer.

"Why lie to your partner?" he asked a few minutes later.

"Because I know he's taken this all on himself."

"Isn't it?" He was in charge of the girl's safety when she'd been captured. In the bodyguard's shoes, Lane would be carrying a ton of guilt on his shoulders.

"Hold up." She tugged on the back of his shirt. "What's your problem with Drake? You don't know him. You don't know our system. Mistakes happen."

"True," he allowed. "My goal isn't to offend you."

"Too late."

That was obvious. "Cassie."

She shoved away from him and started calling Josie's name again.

Great. It wasn't as if he hadn't already dug himself a hole where she was concerned.

No, he didn't know her partner. He had no idea why anyone would grab the girl and then let her get away. But the partner had been posed with that threatening picture. There was no demand for ransom. And those incidents Cassie had listed, while minor on the surface, didn't sound random. Especially when lined up in full context.

His gut instinct insisted there was more to this. That Cassie was a target. He couldn't get the image of that slash over her face out of his mind.

Not that she wanted his help beyond finding her young charge. There wasn't much in the way of a trail at this point. The darkness limited them to a sweep and shout strategy. This place was the textbook definition of isolated. He and Cassie might as well be the only two people in the world. How much worse would a thirteen-year-old be feeling?

Lonely wasn't a familiar sensation, despite the remote corners of the world he'd traveled and the hours he'd spent in a sniper's nest. Rarely had he ever been truly alone. His team had been no further away than a radio call, his location always monitored by someone running overwatch.

"Wait." He held out an arm so Cassie wouldn't blow right past him. "Hear the water? We're close to a waterfall." That meant more places to hide. He crouched down, searching for any sign, and caught a freshly broken twig. "This way." He shouldered through the vegetation, moving closer to the waterfall.

"Josie!"

"Cassie?"

Lane's flashlight painted the girl in a bright light. Cassie rushed by him in a blur to get to the girl. Then she was gently patting Josie down, checking her for injuries as Lane walked up.

The girl's face was marred with dirt, her hair damp and tangled. She seemed a little banged up around the edges with scrapes on her hands and torn pants that revealed a wound on her leg. Overall, she was in one piece. "You are a tough one," he observed.

Her eyes went wide. "Who are you?" She tried to move away, but Cassie held her. "Where's Drake?"

"He's safe. Alive," Cassie replied. "This is Lane. I wouldn't have found you or Drake without his help. Drake is on his way to the hospital."

"What about—" She stopped talking, when Cassie offered her water. After draining the bottle, she started over. "What about the others? Where are they?"

To his surprise, Cassie proceeded with caution. "What others? What do you remember?"

"All of it. We finished one super fun zipline and suddenly they jumped us. Two of them. The tour guide wasn't there. They dragged me off and beat the crap out of Drake." She shuddered and leaned into the hug Cassie offered. "I tried to fight, Cass. I tried. But they tied me so fast and dumped me in one of the 4-by-4s."

"You broke your zip ties," Cassie said. "Way to go."

A small smile brightened the girl's face. "I'm not sure who was more surprised when that worked," she confessed. "But I had the chance, so I ran."

"Where were you going?" Lane asked.

"I wanted to get back to the resort. But when it got dark, I decided to try and find the waterfall because the tour comes out this way almost every day. I figured I wouldn't have to wait long."

As Cassie claimed, the girl was smart and tough. He was more impressed by the minute. "How many people were in the vehicle?" he asked, ignoring Cassie's quelling look.

"Two guys. Older than me, but not as old as Dad."

He saw Cassie register the response. The woman had to be in on it, but they would've had to pick her up on their way to the resort.

"You remember what they looked like?" Cassie asked.

Josie gave a decent description of the men from the photo. When Cassie showed her the picture, she nodded. "That's them. That lady wore a guide's shirt, but she wasn't a real guide."

They would need to have someone follow up and find the real guide stationed at that platform, but he'd leave that to others.

"Did they take your phone?" Cassie asked.

Josie's face fell in disappointment. She shook her head. "I lost it somewhere. I guess when I escaped."

Most likely the men who'd taken her had found the device and kept it, making sure she had no way to call for help. "Let's get out of here," Lane said. His instincts were prickling again. Cassie might not believe the girl was bait, but the hair on the back of his neck disagreed.

On a mission, this was the moment he'd start listening for the throb of helicopter rotors, wondering if the extraction would arrive before any surviving enemies rallied for another shot at them. He guessed a helicopter wasn't an option during a volcanic eruption. Ash clouds and aircraft weren't a good mix. He vaguely recalled all the talk of rerouting commercial air traffic around Iceland when that volcano blew.

"We'll sort it out," Cassie promised as they started back that way. "Your family will be so happy to see you."

"Same."

Lane tuned them out. His focus had shifted. They hadn't discussed it, but he appointed himself head of security now that they'd found Josie. Cassie could ask questions and offer comfort and he'd keep them alive. He was on full alert, their low voices fading into the background while he strained to pick up any hint of what had him on edge.

They had a long hike ahead no matter which route he chose. Having the map in his head, and knowing where they were, he indulged in a brief debate. Best to head back to where he'd left the vehicle Hawk had loaned him. Using the cleared service road would make the trek easier for all of them and there would be cover if they needed it.

He heard movement up ahead. Faint, but definitely there. What he could see of the road was clear, so whoever was out here was hiding in the deep shadows off the path. Could be an animal, but if not, the person had the high ground. What he wouldn't give to have his team backing him up about now. He didn't dare pull his phone and compromise his night vision any further. Should've given Cassie the number for one of his friends. But that only would've helped if they were available and close enough to lend a hand.

Oh, well. The universe didn't offer guarantees and Lane had plenty of practice with creative problem solving. With as little extra movement as possible, he drew his gun and slowed his steps.

"Lane?" Cassie's voice was barely more than a whisper, and right behind him.

Good. Behind him was the safest place to be. "Stay low. Single file."

Creeping forward, each step slow and deliberate, he sought out the threat. What kind of trap had they walked into? Solo attacker or team ambush?

The smartest option for the culprits was to stay near the girl. Observe and wait. Strike if necessary —if Cassie appeared. So why hadn't they attacked immediately? Upon finding Josie, he and Cassie had been distracted. Vulnerable. If the roles were reversed, that's when he would've leapt to the advantage.

Certain games appealed to Lane. Chess. Target practice. Flirting. Football and hockey were a couple more favorites. Hazarding a guess with only partial information? That wasn't entertaining at all.

Just pissed him off.

Suddenly, a red laser sight dusted across the dark leaves of a tree. Lane tucked up close to a thick tree trunk. Cautiously, he followed that light back toward the source until it blinked out. High ground all right, but within range of his SIG. Convenient, once he pinpointed a target.

One shot whizzed by his face and he knew— *knew*—the damned shooter had aimed at Cassie. Since no one screamed, Lane assumed the shooter missed. He leaned around the tree and fired back. Three quick shots, then two more gunshots joined his. From the sound, those shots were from Cassie. In the aftermath of the gunfire, Lane heard a muffled groan and a crash as something fell through the branches, landing hard several yards up the road.

"Wait here," he said as Cassie walked up beside him.

"Hell with that." Her gun was aimed toward the dark road. "We stick together. Josie?"

"Right here."

Lane saw her reach out to touch Cassie's back. "Let me take a look first." He set off before she could argue. If she wanted the girl to see a dead body, that was between them.

He found the shooter, lifeless, in a heap of vegetation just off the road. No sign of the gun. Aiming his flashlight up into the trees, Lane spotted the weapon tangled up with the branches. No one could get to it up there, which was the most relevant issue for Lane.

He knelt down and checked for a pulse. None. He patted the man down and found a knife and a huge flashy handgun better suited to a movie set than any real-life application. In a back pocket, he found a cell phone with a rainbow-sparkle case along with a cell phone in a basic black case. "Hmm. Fascinating style choices," he muttered.

He took control of the weapons before he used his foot to roll the body face up. Definitely dead. Bullet wounds in his chest had bled profusely and either another bullet or the dense trees had taken chunks from his arm, neck and face.

He took several photos with his phone and sent those off to Waylen with a short message about the attack. Then he waved Cassie over.

"That's Greenlee." She swore. "The confirmed man from Welker that we ID'd earlier at the resort."

71

"He's the one who took me away from Drake," Josie added. "Is he… is he dead?"

Cassie moved to block her view of the body. "Yes." She pulled the girl in for a hug and sent Lane a weary look. "Can you notify the police?"

"On it." He sighed.

"What now?" Josie asked.

"We'll have to wait for the police," Cassie explained.

Lane grunted. "That could take some time. Emergency crews are spread thin."

"What do you suggest?" She sat down hard on the road, her shoulders slumped, looking as tired as the girl.

He didn't want to scare Josie, but they couldn't sit out here and wait for someone to come looking for Greenlee. So far, they knew of three people involved in this situation, but there could be more. "I'm going to document the scene and send the info to Hawk."

"Why not the Guardian Agency?" she asked, her brow knitting over that slender nose.

"We can send the intel to them too. The more the merrier. As long as someone with a good reputation with local law enforcement can vouch for us and back up our decisions."

Her frown grew more severe. "What decisions?"

"We're leaving." He cut off her protest with a sharp look. "We are leaving," he repeated. "We're sitting ducks if we stay." Did he have to remind her —out loud—that Josie was in more danger if they waited on law enforcement to show up and take over?

She rolled to her feet. "You're right. But I don't have to like it."

A snappy comeback danced on the tip of his tongue, a promise of something she might like better. He managed to keep the suggestion locked down. There was a kid present. They started moving and one of the flashlights swept over her. "Hold up. You're hurt."

"I'm not." She followed his gaze, knocking his hand away when he reached for her. "What are you doing?"

He kept his hands to himself, barely. She'd been hit, damn it. "Greenlee tagged you."

"Let me see." Josie inserted herself between them. Holding the flashlight for Cassie to get a better look. "Shirt's trashed," the girl declared. "But you're not bleeding."

Lane wanted to confirm that assessment with his own eyes, but this wasn't the time or place. At best, Cassie was a colleague, despite his hope that she'd agree to have drinks with him sometime. At worst, she was still a target. "Let's get moving."

Cassie grumbled as they hiked on. "This was one of my favorite shirts. Dang it."

Lane made a silent promise to replace the shirt

at the first opportunity. It was his fault the shooter had gotten so close. He should've been quicker. Chosen a different route. Done something less predictable.

"Hey." Her hand brushed over his arm as she matched his pace. Her skin was warm. Soft. But it was the strength he could feel in her hand that fascinated him. She was a woman with every wonderful feminine attribute, but she was brave and tough, and a damn good shot.

"It's not your fault," she murmured, her voice barely audible over his heavy footsteps.

He had a different opinion.

"Lane? Did you hear me?"

"I did."

"And?"

He glanced down, wishing he could see her better. Her features were cast in shadows. "What? I heard you," he said.

"You disagree."

"Yes." He absolutely did. "You called Hawk for help and—" And he'd let her get hurt. Not acceptable.

"And you gave it," she said. "Thank you. I couldn't have found Josie without you."

The tightness in his chest eased. "You're welcome. Sorry about your shirt."

She made a sound that might've been a laugh.

"Might be fun to see what happens if I send a bill to Welker Specialists."

"Fun?" His temper simmered. Everything was pointing to that group being rotten. He didn't know who they were or why they were messing with her and the people under her protection, but damned if he'd let her deal with it alone. "Keep me in the loop on that. Please," he added when she didn't reply.

"Seriously?"

"Seriously." He had a company name and a dead employee. It wasn't much, but it was a start. Definitely enough to ask Waylen to help him research. Whatever Cassie decided to do next, Lane intended to be her shadow until he was convinced she was well and truly safe.

She wouldn't lose another shirt—or anything else—on his watch.

5

*C*assie was exhausted by the time the Knowles family was reunited. Walking into the suite with Josie had been akin to entering an emotional tornado of gratitude and relief. It was a beautiful moment for Josie, a testament to both her courage and how much she was loved.

Cassie and Lane let Josie tell her tale. The girl glossed over the more dangerous aspects of the search and rescue. Everyone gave kudos to the nanny for her quick thinking when it came to the photo. An image the police would be asking for soon. Unless Claudia was dealing with those details.

Cassie needed to send in her preliminary report, with all those details they hadn't burdened the family with. And she would, just as soon as she confirmed that Drake was all right.

The family put Lane through a gauntlet of hugs

and praises just as intense as the affection showered on Cassie and Josie.

Cassie loved this family. So much. She felt closer to the Knowles than she did to her own relatives back in Iowa. And she had to confirm that the protection plan for them was solid before she made her exit to clean up and get some rest.

She spoke with the protection team that had taken over so she could search. The two men confirmed that aside from worry over Josie, nothing untoward had happened in her absence. Together, the three of them gathered around the table and called the Chicago office. Arrangements were quickly made to move the family to a safe location. Additional personnel were also coming in to assist until they understood the impetus behind the kidnapping. The logistics would be tricky, considering the crisis created by the volcano, but Judith and Dave remained confident in the Guardian Agency.

That warmed Cassie's heart as much as anything else. It was important to her to do a good job and represent her agency well.

"You've gone above and beyond, Cassie," Nolan Swann's voice came through the speaker. As a managing partner of the elite protection firm, his praise was welcome.

"Thank you," she replied. "I've had good help."

With an effort, she kept her gaze from wandering toward the door where Lane waited.

For her?

That was odd. He should be gone by now. They weren't actually a team. His assistance had been appreciated, but his part was done. Who was she kidding? He'd been invaluable out there and she did want a chance to thank him personally.

As soon as this call was done, she'd do that and send him back to Hawk.

"We're relieving you for a few days," Swann continued. "Take some time to rest up. We'll talk again tomorrow afternoon when we have more information."

"Yes, sir," Cassie was floored, but the response to his authority was automatic.

She stared at the phone, hoping no one else could see her internal struggle. Her chest went tight as she resisted the order. This couldn't be happening. The Knowles family was *her* case. Her people. Her responsibility. She'd been with them from the start. There hadn't been a single scenario in her mind in which she walked away.

Everything inside her wanted to protest, but she couldn't do it. Not with everyone here.

She'd never been pulled from a case before. What did this mean? The Guardian Agency didn't make a move without cause and thoughtful reasoning.

Her mind spun. Where had she screwed up? What did they know that she didn't?

When the plans were set, Swann ended the call and Cassie pushed back from the table. She endured another round of hugs from the family, wishing them the best and promising to stay in touch.

Assuming that was allowed. She'd ask Claudia about the protocol in these situations.

The last few months of her life had been interwoven with these four wonderful people. As she left their suite, she felt as if she'd been set adrift.

Did that make her clingy? Maybe Swann feared she'd grown too close to be an effective protector.

"You didn't do anything wrong."

She turned toward the source of the softly-spoken words and saw Lane. He hovered a few feet behind her. In her shock, she'd walked right by him. Swann might have a good reason to be concerned, after all.

"I'd like to believe you." She moved toward her room, across the hall and a few doors down from the Knowles's suite.

"Then do that."

She swallowed hard as she passed Drake's door. "Why are you following me? I'm in no mood to flirt or go for drinks." In fact, as soon as she washed off the grime of the search, she was heading to the hospital.

"You want to see your partner," Lane said. "I can drive."

In her pocket, her phone chimed, but she ignored the alert. "I'll drive myself when I'm ready."

He leaned one of those firm shoulders against the wall, his gaze unrelenting. "Then I call shotgun."

"Go away, Lane." She shook her head. "No, wait." She couldn't send him away without keeping her promise to herself. Staring at him, she tried to get the words in the right order.

"I'm waiting."

She looked up and down the hallway. Inviting him inside her room wasn't an option. Guards were posted near the elevator, the closest stairwell, and right outside the Knowles family suite. She didn't need word getting back to her agency or his that he'd joined her in her room.

"I appreciate you," she began, her voice barely more than a whisper. "Thank you for your help tonight."

His eyebrows, several shades darker than his hair, arched upward. "You don't say."

She ignored that in favor of being the mature adult in this conversation. "I appreciate you," she repeated. "You were a big help to me, Lane. Without you I might still be searching for Josie and Drake."

He scowled, apparently unimpressed with her gratitude. "That's quite a sendoff."

"I mean it," she insisted. She rested her fingertips on the warm skin of his forearm, hoping no one noticed the contact. "Thank you."

"I'm not standing here for your gratitude."

He might as well have dumped ice water over her head. Unhappier than she had any business feeling over a man she barely knew, she turned away and tapped the card to the lock. "Then go. I'll let Hawk know you were everything I needed," she snapped, shoving open her door.

He tried to follow her, crowding her through the doorway, but he didn't come all the way inside. "You didn't tell them about that picture you received."

She hauled him inside and let the door close behind him. "Is that why you're hovering? It's not an issue." His lips parted, ready to argue. "If it becomes an issue, I can take care of myself."

"Why hide that kind of threat from your bosses?"

"I didn't hide it." She'd meant to forward the photo to Claudia. "I didn't mention it back there because it could've upset the client. And I have more important things on my mind," she shot back. "Besides, my tech assistant has access to my phone. She's probably already working on it." It could even be why she'd been removed from the protection detail. Swann had said they would talk more.

"You're in danger." Lane's eyes dropped to her lips, then lifted away to scan the room behind her.

After their trek through the forest, she wouldn't blame him if his interest in her had faded. She folded her arms. "I could say the same about you." He didn't take the hint, standing firm. "Leave, Lane." Couldn't get clearer than that. "I'm fine." Or she would be soon. Shower, clean clothes, and seeing Drake would go a long way to restoring her balance.

He shouldered past her. "Lane!"

"Does your group always leave their employees to fight solo?"

"Never." She'd always felt as if she were part of a team. "That's not what's happening here." Gamble and Swann would never leave her hanging out to dry. "That picture was a stunt, a diversion to throw off my search for Josie."

He turned on the overhead light. "She was kidnapped to draw you out."

It took a second for her to understand the scene. Her room had been searched. It didn't make any sense at all. The contents of her suitcase had been dumped on the bed. She didn't usually unpack into hotel dressers or closets, preferring to keep her belongings contained. Made it easier if she ever needed to leave in a hurry.

"Anything missing?"

"Yes." Stifling the urge to scream in frustration, she pulled out her phone. "My laptop is gone. It was on the desk."

She took pictures of the room, making sure Lane wasn't in any of them, and sent the photos on to Claudia with a text message.

While she waited for the call back, she debated calling the police.

"Call the cops," Lane said.

"No, thanks," she disagreed. "They have bigger issues to deal with right now."

He rolled his eyes, but didn't argue with her.

Her cell phone rang and he turned away, taking a look at the sliding glass door. Cassie wasn't expecting to see Swann's name and number on the caller ID. Braced for the worst, she answered.

"Are you injured?" he asked.

"No, sir. I'm fine." It was true, as long as she didn't think about Lane being here in her personal space that was dominated by a bed. "I took every precau—"

"You're not at fault, Cassie," Swann said, cutting off her apology. "No one thinks that. In fact, I called because Claudia is already tracking down the laptop."

Cassie was so tired, she'd forgotten the company computers had tracking devices. "Good. What can I do to help?"

From across the room, she heard Lane muttering. She didn't need his permission or approval on this. It was her life, her career. And if Swann gave her a task, she'd follow through. She loved her company and wanted to keep her job.

"Pack up your belongings, change rooms, and get some sleep."

Cassie sank into the nearest chair, avoiding eye contact with Lane. Change rooms? If this one had been searched, couldn't she just stay? Her mind was reeling and she was pretty sure she had the logic wrong, but… "Pardon me?"

"You're exhausted," Swann said, his voice filled with kindness and concern. "The police are overextended with the volcano emergency. And honestly, this break in and theft isn't something I want to advertise."

"Of course not." That much she understood. Did she dare mention the Welker Specialists connection? "Sir, we never received a ransom for Josie." It had been one of the first details she'd planned to share in her preliminary report. The report she couldn't file so easily now without her laptop.

"Tell him the rest," Lane ordered in a whisper.

"I've been wondering about that too," Swann said. "Getting you out of the resort gave them easier access to your room and the laptop. Is there a connection to you that we need to explore?"

She cringed. Everything a hacker might want was on that laptop, from her personal banking information to the itinerary for Judith and her family. She didn't need to point out that she followed all the recommended security protocols. If someone skilled enough wanted access, they would find a way. "I don't suppose it was just a stunt to inconvenience the agency?"

Swann made a humming sound.

"Tell him the rest," Lane said, loud enough to be overheard this time.

"You're not alone."

Cassie knew by the tone that Swann wasn't pleased that she'd hidden that detail. Cassie glared at Lane. If he got her fired, she'd wring his neck. "No, sir. Lane Benning is here."

"That's the scout Hawk sent over to help you search for Josie."

"Yes, sir." No surprise that Swann knew about Lane, Hawk, or anything else. The Brotherhood Protectors and the Guardian Agency had a history of cooperation. "He's concerned for my safety." She closed her eyes. "During the search I received a text with an image of Drake on the ground." She had to swallow the emotion before she could explain the rest of it. "I meant to forward the message to Claudia."

"Hold on."

The line went silent on the other end.

"What did he say?" Lane demanded.

"He put me on hold." She was too weary to kick him out or tell him it wasn't his business. She tapped the speaker button and set the phone down so she could pack her suitcase.

"What are you doing?" Lane asked, whispering once more.

"Now you're discreet." She rolled her eyes. "I've been ordered to change rooms."

"Good." He reached to help with her clothing and she swatted his hand away. "You'll move to my room."

She froze, startled speechless by the absurd suggestion. "Not an option," she said.

"Cassie!" Swann's voice intruded, vibrating with urgency. "Tell Claudia you give her permission to access that message with the threatening photo."

"It's your personal device," Claudia explained, in an arch tone. "And I value our privacy policy. Since you're not incapacitated, we require consent."

"You have my permission," Cassie said, smothering an untimely urge to laugh. Claudia was a stickler for the details because she was so good at what she did. That was one of the things that made her invaluable, even when her integrity frustrated the boss.

The thought gave Cassie some comfort in the midst of yet another layer in this crisis. If the tech and research expert could speak her mind without worrying about getting fired, Cassie could do the same. Before she could bring up the idea of staying put, Swann swore.

She scrambled to take him off speaker, but Lane grabbed the phone first.

"Bad isn't it?" he asked.

"Yes," Swann replied, completely ignoring that Lane shouldn't be privy to any of this. "In this image Drake looks dead."

"Whoever did this didn't think we'd ever find him," Cassie admitted. "Without Lane, we wouldn't have," she added.

"Drake is too tough for that." Swann's voice was rough around the edges. "He would've found his way out eventually." He cleared his throat. "The bigger issue is the obvious threat to you. We'll dig in, of course, but it's hard to believe they only wanted to nab your laptop."

"My thoughts exactly," Lane chimed in.

Under different circumstances, she might give him points for not being cowed in the slightest by her obvious displeasure. At the moment, she was irritated as hell. They were railroading her and she needed to remind them she was a force all on her own. "Please dig into Welker," she said. "Their man Greenlee was behind the ambush after we'd found Josie."

"And he didn't fire at the girl," Lane added.

Cassie fumed. When this call was over, she was

going to rip Lane apart. She was the lead—or had been. She wasn't only well-trained and capable, she'd demonstrated her skills time and again. Whatever he was doing, inserting himself into her life this way, was completely unnecessary.

"Claudia knows that Greenlee was also seen here at the resort before we went out to search," Cassie said.

Swann's sigh was heavy. "Welker Specialists doesn't have the cleanest reputation, but this is…" His voice trailed off. "This is a serious breach if the incidents are connected."

Cassie was well-aware of that. Along with the fact that there didn't seem to be any motive for Welker to be involved in any of this. And she couldn't think of any reason for them to target her. "What if Greenlee was freelancing?"

Another sigh from the speaker.

Lane asked the question that was at the forefront of her mind. "Who wants Cassie dead?"

"We'll find out," Swann promised. "Cassie, keep a low profile until we can get you out of Hawaii."

"I'd rather not leave my assignment." It was her last ditch effort to stay with the Knowles family.

"Even if you're a threat to them?" Swann queried gently.

The sympathy in his voice touched her. "Well, obviously no. I don't want that."

She'd studied and trained, mentally and physically, for her role with the Guardian Agency. Her job was to protect others, to prevent trouble, not to multiply the risks. She glanced at Lane, wishing he wasn't standing there, staring her down like he knew how she felt.

He couldn't possibly.

Well, that was blatantly untrue. As a SEAL, Lane would've worked with high-caliber teams, the military's elite. No way anyone survived a career like that without making a few mistakes and picking up plenty of scars, inside and out.

"Can I go check on Drake?" she asked.

"I'd rather you didn't go out alone," Swann replied.

She opened her mouth, ready to fight on this point. No way they would keep her locked in a hotel room, away from everything until they deemed it safe. That was madness. She'd have cabin-fever within a day. There had to be another option. If she couldn't help the Knowles family, she could surely be useful somewhere. The island was in a state of emergency. They couldn't expect her to hide until it was possible to leave. She was about to suggest she head toward Hawk's operation when Lane cut her off.

"I'll be with her."

"What?" she blurted. "No. No he won't."

"You have the time?" Swann asked over her objection.

"I do."

She suppressed a shiver as those two little words seemed to reverberate through the room. What was happening? He held her gaze as if he was making a personal vow. "I can take care of myself," she reminded both men.

It had been years since she'd actually *needed* a man's strength or protection. Years. Back when she'd been a teenager on the farm in Iowa. Yes, Lane had taken the lead a few hours ago, stepping between her and Greenlee, but her aim had been as true as his. Cooperation and teamwork were important. Despite her independence, she considered those traits essential in a working relationship. But this conversation felt more like she was losing ground, as if Swann was dumping her with a babysitter.

"Your background checks out," Swann was saying. "We appreciate the assistance while we get to the bottom of this. I'll expect daily updates. Be safe."

The call ended and Lane held out the cell phone. "You're pissed."

"You better believe it," she snapped. "I can—"

"Take care of yourself, I know." He didn't look pleased about it.

She returned to her packing. Not her job to manage his feelings. She had her hands full with her own. Pride bruised, she zipped up her suitcase, avoiding his gaze. "If you know, why... Why did you do that to me?"

"Because you need protection too."

She resisted that with every fiber of her being. Exhausted or not, she could take care of herself. Especially in this case. There wasn't any reason to target her. It had to be blatant intimidation, nothing more.

In the mirror, she caught a reflection of her scorched shirt and the mild burn on her arm. That was more than intimidation. She didn't want to agree with him. "I'm not staying in your room." She didn't trust herself not to do something ridiculous, like kiss him.

"You are." He pressed a keycard into her hands and gave her the room number. "I can clear my stuff and crash with one of the guys."

Oh, that could work. "Waylen or Kian?"

He shrugged. "Harlan or Raider wouldn't lock me out either."

She admired Lane's connections. The man had good friends. Friends who had responded in a hurry to help Drake. "Keep your room." She handed the keycard back to him. "I'll go to the ranch and check in with Hawk. At least there I can stay off the radar without being bored."

"Not a bad solution." He folded his arms, watching her.

He probably expected her to swoon over the

flexing biceps. And okay, a little part of her was all too willing to do just that. Lane was striking with his pale eyes, chiseled jaw, and a hint of a smile always on his lips.

She did *not* need to be thinking about his lips. But she continued staring, blaming the gaffe on weariness.

"How about this?" His voice was gentle. "I'll take you to my room so you can clean up. Then we'll go to the hospital and see your friend. After that, we'll decide what's next."

She hesitated.

"Would you rather stay here?"

It wouldn't be the smart move considering she had orders to leave. "Fine." She tugged the suitcase along behind her as she headed for the door.

She had to compartmentalize and focus on the big picture. That's all. Drake mattered a whole lot more than where she showered or slept. Figuring out why Greenlee had ambushed them—and taken aim at her—was far more important than her misgivings about being with Lane.

They were both professionals and, right now, he was the only one behaving accordingly.

6

$\mathcal{L}$ ane couldn't believe his luck that Cassie's boss had sided with him. Now, instead of being pushy, he was simply doing the job. Protecting her.

Of course, that meant surviving his vivid imagination while she showered in the bathroom they would now share. Out on the beach, her swimwear had showcased her body to perfection, leaving Lane craving more. He coveted the details. He wanted all her secrets, personally and intimately. And he was willing to share his secrets with her.

Best to keep all that lust and desire locked down until she trusted him. He hadn't exactly lied about crashing with one of his pals, but he had no intention of leaving her alone here or anywhere else. Not after the ambush.

He respected her independence. Found it

damned attractive. Under any other circumstances, he'd honor it. But he'd promised her boss that he'd keep her safe. If Lane knew anything, it was how to keep a vow, big or small.

This particular promise felt nearly as big as the oath he'd given his country way back in his twenties. Nearly as right as the words he'd recited on that day.

He knew better than to second guess his instincts. What started as a flirtation had become important. He didn't understand it entirely. Couldn't explain it any better. He didn't even care that it didn't make sense to feel this obligation to a woman he barely knew.

When listening to the shower became too overwhelming, he distracted himself and checked in with Hawk first, then Waylen, bringing them up to speed. Hawk wasn't exactly thrilled that he'd left a body out there on the zipline trail. Lane endured the dressing down and promised to cooperate with police when the time came.

Waylen wasn't much more understanding. "What the hell were you thinking?" he demanded. "The cops might charge you for leaving that scene."

"Y'know, Cassie's boss didn't give her as much crap as you're dishing out," Lane said. "We had to protect the kidnap victim."

"Her boss probably looked at your record and

counted the fact that you called it in at all as progress."

"Shut up." They both knew he'd been good at his job. "What did you learn about this Greenlee guy? Any connections here in Hawaii?"

Waylen swore under his breath. "He arrived, alone, two days ago. Commercial flight. Give me some time with it."

Lane knew better than to push too hard. No one liked a nag. And no disrespect to Cassie's agency, but he'd put his money on Waylen. "Our next stop is the hospital. Did you get a read on her partner?"

"Not much to read," Waylen replied. "He passed out a couple of times on the ride over. He didn't have the energy for a chat. At the ER, the nurse took one look at him and rushed him back for treatment. I'm not sure what you think you'll get out of him."

That was the thing about his friends—they knew him well. "We're gonna try anyway."

"We?" Waylen moved on before Lane had to come up with an answer. "Tread lightly," he warned. "It's obvious she cares about her partner."

A credit to Cassie, in Lane's opinion. But they needed answers and he didn't share her confidence in Drake's innocence. Not yet, anyway. Someone wanted her out of the way for some reason and right now, Drake was the only player with a clear motive.

"Maybe she more than cares," Waylen suggested.

Lane bit back the instant denial that would give his friend too much information. "Could be," he said as if Cassie's romantic inclinations were of no importance.

Waylen busted out laughing. "You've got it bad for a woman you just met."

"Could be," he repeated. Why argue? He heard the taps shut off in the bathroom. "Gotta run. Let me know what you find."

He ended the call before Waylen could land another verbal jab.

Cassie emerged a few minutes later, dressed in loose pants and a t-shirt sporting the logo for a popular surfboard company. The neckline had been shaped to show her cleavage to the best advantage. Lane loved Hawaii more and more.

Her dark hair was damp, parted in the middle and pushed back from her face, curling as it cascaded past her shoulders. His fingers tingled, desperate to touch those silky waves.

"Give me five minutes." He started past her, breathing in the warm scent of her skin. He wanted a taste, one little kiss, so damn bad. *Timing*, he reminded himself ruthlessly. Pushing her would only set him back from the end goal of winning her over.

"Lane." She stopped him with a gentle touch to his arm.

He froze, trapped by the lust pulsing through his system. In her eyes, he saw what might be an echo of the need he felt. *Timing.* She needed to see her partner and he intended to get her through that visit safely. "You can't go alone." He managed to squeeze out the words through a throat gone dry. "Five minutes."

"Mm." She didn't remove her hand. "Okay." Her head bowed, her gaze on the place where they touched.

He couldn't be expected to break the sweet contact. That was asking too much. The craving for her thundered in his chest. He was lost to her. "Cassie?"

She looked up, a soft smile teasing those lush, rosy lips. "I'll wait."

He was ready now. Ready to devour her. But she was clean and fresh while he felt grimy from their trek through the rainforest. When they kissed—and he prayed he wouldn't have to wait much longer—he wanted it to be memorable for all the right reasons.

At last, she released him. His entire being demanded that he follow her, but he forced himself toward the shower instead.

He hustled, more than a little concerned she'd take off without him anyway. Trust was a two-way street and he had to extend a little if he hoped to gain any from her. He felt a surge of relief when he came out of the bathroom to find her curled up in the chair near the glass door. She'd braided her wet hair back from her face.

He had two minutes left and he didn't waste them, grabbing his clothes and stepping out of sight to dress. After running his hands through his hair, he moved to the closet and slipped on a pair of deck shoes.

"Ready?" She looked up from her cell phone, her face somber, her skin pale. He'd expected her to be pacing by the door, impatient to get moving. "Is there a problem?"

Frowning, she held out her phone. "Take a look."

He crossed the room, a frisson of dread prickling along his skin. Ignoring the device in her hand, he sat down on the edge of the bed. "Tell me."

"Claudia sent me an image from the CCTV here at the resort." She put the phone down firmly on the table. "Drake and Greenlee." She swore. "They were alone, back near the kitchens. Night before last." Her eyes were brimming with tears. "It can't be what it looks like, can it?"

Though he hadn't seen the photo, he was afraid it was exactly what it looked like. "Did Claudia give you any context?"

"Not yet." Cassie tucked her arms around her middle. "And what context is there? Greenlee's dead. Drake can say whatever he wants about the meeting. Who's left to confirm the truth?"

"He can't possibly know Greenlee's dead."

A flicker of hope lit up her gaze. "Good point. We need a strategy."

"What happened to all your confidence in your partner's integrity?" He didn't know why he was defending the man now, when he'd been the number-one skeptic earlier.

She pointed at the phone. "The picture. If it wasn't real, Claudia wouldn't have sent it."

"Would you forward it to Waylen? Please?"

She shoved herself up and out of the chair. "I don't need more of the 'your team's better than mine' routine."

He watched her walk toward the door and back again. She made a couple of trips before he realized she was still barefoot. Her feet were adorable, her toenails painted in a shimmering aqua color. "I have a better idea," he declared.

Pausing, she studied him. "I'm all ears."

"Let's go to the hospital and see your friend." He held up a hand when she started to interrupt. "No questions, just a simple welfare check. Then we'll swing by a bar I know and grab a beer." Standing, he closed the distance, making himself available in case she wanted to touch him again. "After that, we'll come back here, get some rest, and plan our next move."

"Lane." Her eyes were wide and lovely, despite the dark circles underneath.

"You need rest. Time to recover. Just getting to Drake's room at this hour will be a challenge. Let's save the interrogation for tomorrow."

She sighed. "Odds are good you and I will be on the hot seat tomorrow for leaving Greenlee out there."

"We can burn down that bridge tomorrow." Why wouldn't she touch him? He was right here, well within reach. "What do you say?"

Her chin bobbed in the affirmative. "It's a good plan." At last she reached out, squeezed his hand. "Thanks, Lane."

Timing and patience. He expected more resistance from her before they returned to the room, but this was good progress. While she slipped on a pair of canvas shoes, he grabbed the keys to the vehicle he'd borrowed from Hawk and they headed out.

Outside the air felt thick and smelled worse from the ash cloud hovering over the island. He glanced up, sad to see the glittering stars of previous nights blotted out. When they reached the borrowed Jeep, he opened the door for her. "My favorite ops were at night," he said, overcome with a sudden nostalgia for his career.

Being a SEAL had been damned hard work most days. In some ways, the easiest part was being the tip of the spear, out there executing orders with precision. Lane preferred doing a task over making the decisions and tough calls. Yes, operations were demanding, often with complex terrain to overcome in addition to the mission objective. But as a SEAL, once he had those orders, he knew his role. His purpose was clear.

As a team, they had a goal and they worked to achieve it.

Now, retired, he lacked that intense focus. Although he enjoyed all the traveling and downtime, part of him was getting antsy about the next step. He couldn't see it clearly. That sense of the unknown was disconcerting for a man who'd been told where to train, where to live, and where to work for the past couple of decades.

"Night vision goggles are that much fun?"

He laughed. "They are pretty cool," he agreed as he buckled into the driver's seat. "I was just thinking about those moments, before or after the action, when I'd look up into a sea of stars."

"That must've been action in remote places."

"Absolutely." He grinned. "I loved being reminded how big the world is." He pulled away from the resort. "Stars are brighter out here. Usually."

"Usually," she agreed, bracing an elbow on the open edge of the windowless door. "My dad taught me about the constellations. It's corny, I know, but

I'm always a little lonely when I can't spot the North Star."

"Where did he teach you?" Lane would tread lightly, but he wouldn't miss this chance to learn more while she was in a mood to share.

"Iowa." Her voice sounded as wistful as he felt. "Middle of nowhere farm country. Lots of stars. Growing up, our weather warnings were mostly for blizzards and ice," she said. "With decent lead time to prepare. Never thought I'd miss blizzards and ice."

He waited, expecting her to ask about his hometown. Should've known she was too distracted. Or maybe he really was wasting his time and she wasn't interested. Glancing over, he caught her staring at him. Was he imagining the curiosity and the heat in her gaze?

"You can ask me anything," he offered. "For you, I'm an open book."

He heard a soft snort. "For a woman, you mean."

"No." Although he enjoyed women, he didn't enjoy opening up with women. Or anyone else for that matter. "For you." He stopped for the traffic light and smiled at her. "Don't ask me to explain it. So far, I can't figure it out." He shrugged. "Aside from the obvious."

"The obvious?"

"You're special, Cassie."

She looked away and, unfortunately, didn't ask him anything. He honored the silence, despite his urge to share every damn secret he had with her. He chalked it up to stress. More than the search for Josie, there seemed to be an energy simmering up from the island itself. A generalized anxiety pressed in on them from every angle and it only intensified as they approached the hospital.

She didn't speak again until they were walking inside the facility.

At the information desk staffed by two security guards, they were warned visiting hours were over. Linking her hand with his, Cassie pleaded, telling the guards she was Drake's sister and had just learned that he'd been admitted. Lane was impressed with both the tactic and the convincing delivery.

Armed with Drake's room number and a warning not to stay long, they hurried down the hall to the elevators.

"Nicely done," he said when they were alone. He didn't point out that she could release his hand. He was enjoying the contact too much.

"Are you upset I lied? Disappointed?"

"Not a bit. Impressed. Sincerely," he added when she gave him a doubtful side eye.

Her eyebrows flexed and she took a deep breath as the doors opened. "Check in only. Interrogation tomorrow," she murmured.

Cassie was determined, and from what he'd seen, nearly unstoppable when she set her mind on a goal. He buried the grin. As much as he enjoyed getting acquainted, her mind was on the situation and the welfare of her partner.

She marched down the hall, pausing when they reached Drake's room. The door was open slightly, and from what Lane could see, the room was dark. Quiet too, aside from the typical soft noises from medical equipment.

He gave her hand a squeeze. "Check in only," he whispered at her ear.

Rolling her shoulders back, she eased inside. Her tight grip on his hand was the only clue that she was uncertain. Drake was alone, the other bed in the room was empty. Eyes closed, his breathing was slow and steady.

They'd cleaned him up and he had stitches from his eyebrow to his hairline, across his cheek, and along his jaw. Lane knew from experience that the bruises would take time to fade and scarring was inevitable.

Cassie released his hand and moved closer to her friend. Tenderly, she smoothed Drake's hair back and gently kissed his forehead.

Suddenly, Drake reacted, throwing an arm up to protect himself. Lane surged forward, blocking Drake's strike and pushing Cassie back, out of the way. "Easy, man," he said in the most soothing tone he could manage. "Easy."

"What the…" Drake's voice trailed off when he saw Cassie. "Cass? Thought—" He cleared his throat. "Crap. I thought you were here to kill me."

She wedged herself back in front of Lane, her hip snug against his thigh. "Me personally, or someone in general?"

To Lane's shock, the man started crying. "Greenlee." He swore, swiping at the tears rolling down his face. "It's Greenlee. You have to get out of here, Cass. Go."

She patted Drake's shoulder. "Why would Greenlee be trying to kill you?"

Lane gave her points for composure. He was ready to get her as far away from Hawaii as possible. Anything to keep her safe.

"Go!" Drake's monitors started beeping faster. He pleaded with Lane, "Thank your pals for saving me. Now get her out of here."

"I need answers, Drake."

A nurse hurried in, and seeing Cassie and Lane, she glared. "Visiting hours are over."

"My brother—"

"Needs his rest." She clearly wouldn't be swayed as easily as the guards downstairs. "We'll see you tomorrow."

Lane ushered Cassie out of the room, letting the

nurse get Drake settled. "We checked on him," he reminded her. "And you need rest too."

"You promised me a beer first."

He managed not to roll his eyes. "I did, yes. Come on."

She rocked on her feet while they waited for the elevator. "I don't want to leave him when he's scared."

He understood. Whatever her partner was up to, Lane didn't think that reaction had been faked. "We can't stay." Her story would only hold up so long. "Tell your assistant or whoever to keep an eye on him."

She chewed on her lip. Refused to get into the elevator when it arrived.

"I'll toss you over my shoulder," he threatened.

"Fine." She stomped into the elevator.

"Greenlee can't hurt him," he reminded her. "Any accomplices will be searching for their missing hired gun. And we'll be back in the morning."

She rubbed her eyes. "Promise?"

Lane took a breath. He wouldn't make a promise just to break it come daybreak. "Barring any more trouble, yes, I promise."

"Thanks." As soon as they exited the elevator, she started texting, her full attention on the messages she was firing off.

With one hand on the small of her back, he guided her out to the car. His mind was spinning with scenarios, none of them comforting. The incidents Cassie had told him about were disconcerting. Adding in the atypical kidnapping, the ambush, and her stolen laptop led him to one conclusion: she was in serious danger.

Lane needed the who and the why as soon as possible. He wanted Waylen's take on this situation as much as Cassie wanted the opinion of her team. If he had any luck left, his friend would still be at the bar when they got there.

'll let you know when I find something.

Cassie waited and waited for the follow up, but Claudia was apparently done texting for now. It was almost eleven local time which made it… Cassie sighed. She had no idea what time it was in Chicago, headquarters of the Guardian Agency. The math was just beyond her right now. It might not even matter. Claudia worked remotely and probably lived somewhere else.

Cassie was so tired.

And weary of the growing list of unanswered questions.

The sweet, clear island breezes were gone, tempered by the ash cloud that seemed to get worse every time she stepped outside. Maybe it wouldn't be that hard to follow Swann's order to lay low after all.

Pocketing her phone, she shifted to study Lane. "You have quick moves," she observed.

"Thanks for noticing." He tossed her that carefree smile and suddenly the poor air quality and weariness faded out of her mind.

The man was hot. Along with all the other attributes she shouldn't be noticing, she appreciated his protective streak, even if she didn't really need his direct and persistent intervention. "Do you always care this much?"

"No." Another grin while he waited for the traffic light to change. "As I said, you're special."

"Hmm." The light turned green and he pulled forward. Did she dare trust those words? "Where are we going?"

"A bar my buddies and I stumbled on. Quirky and local, hence the name. Good beer. Excellent nachos. Pool and darts, if you're in the mood."

"You're serious." They were just going out to a neighborhood bar? That felt weird and significant and couldn't possibly be either of those things. She was overtired and overthinking.

"You don't like quirky?"

She saw him check his mirrors as he slowed for the next turn. Resisting the urge to swivel around and look behind them, she said. "Quirky has its place."

"What about pool?"

She shook her head. "Pool is fun. Maybe not

tonight." She wasn't sure she had the energy for anything more than drinking a beer right now.

"Agreeing to a second date, already. Nice," he teased. "Relax. I won't hold you to that. I figured some time to unwind would help before we call it a night." Again, his eyes cycled through the mirrors.

She eyed the road ahead. They'd left the brighter lights and busier streets near the resort behind. "Are we being followed?"

"Yes." His fingers stretched and curled around the steering wheel. "Not much room to hide out here."

If the driver following them tried anything, Lane would be forced into the trees that grew right up to the road. "The bar is close?"

He lifted his chin. "Right around that corner."

She eyed the bend in the road with more than a little dread. There didn't seem to be anything but air on the other side. "Be careful."

"Always."

Everything about him appeared relaxed. Shoulders, hands, legs. Everything but his jaw, she noticed with a smidge of relief. *That's* where he hid his tension, behind a short beard and that disarming smile. Good to know.

"Any chance they're just headed to the same bar?"

"Anything is possible." He navigated the turn,

taking a deep breath once they were through it without incident.

She was grateful for the dark, suspecting a steep drop off was on the other side of that curve. At least she wouldn't learn the hard way tonight.

As stated, the bar came into view and Lane pulled into the parking area. The car tailing them drove on by. She tried and failed to get anything more than the make and model. "No idea on the plates," she said.

"No worries." He squeezed into a space as close to the front door as he could manage. "They won't bother us here. Assuming they were actually tailing us."

Her gut said they were, but it seemed counter-productive to dwell on it. He'd brought her here to relax. She eyed the bar as they walked inside. Wood gleamed, burnished gold in the low light. Colorful island decor ranging from Tiki masks to surf boards were mounted on the walls. Music pumped from a jukebox tucked back by the bar. Even at this hour, all the barstools were filled as were most of the tables both inside and out under the covered patio. "How did you find this place?"

He laced his fingers through hers. "My friend, Raider, has a knack for finding things. Including places like this one."

She could see there was more to the story, but he

was leading her to a table where the friends who'd helped Drake were seated.

"Make room." Land tipped his head, suggesting Waylen move over to the bench with Kian.

Kian laughed while Waylen grudgingly obliged.

Lane urged her into the vacated seat. "Any beer allergies?"

She laughed. "Any and all IPAs will land in your lap."

"Noted." With a wink, he strode away to the bar.

For a moment, she was at a loss, facing Lane's friends. "Thanks for your help with Drake," she said at last. "I hope I'm not intruding here."

Kian's gaze narrowed as he studied her. "Waylen? Am I drunk or hallucinating?"

Waylen smirked. "Neither." He elbowed his friend. "Be polite."

"I'm always polite."

"I take it you guys don't usually bring strangers to your favorite place to unwind?" she queried.

Kian continued to stare as if she'd turned into a unicorn. "No." He exchanged a look with Waylen. "Not the norm."

She wasn't sure if he was referring to her, Lane, or the situation as a whole. It didn't matter.

"We found this spot a few days ago," Waylen explained.

"When we got tired of paying resort prices for a

pint," Kian added. He leaned forward. "So you're Lane's new assignment? He sent a text."

"Seems so," she said. "My vote against gaining a bodyguard didn't count."

"Or maybe the risks are more serious than you think," Waylen said.

Drake's fear of Greenlee came to mind. "Maybe." She caught sight of Lane returning. "Either way, I'm sorry if my trouble wrecked your vacation."

Waylen shook his head. "We're blaming that on the volcano. That's what the locals are doing."

Lane set down the beers and slid in beside her until his leg was pressed against hers. "It's a lager from a local craft brewery."

"Perfect. Thanks."

As the conversation progressed from the immediate crisis of the erupting volcano, she learned Lane had retired with four other SEALs and the five of them had been traveling for several months. It sounded as if they all enjoyed being tourists. Even—or especially—while hanging out in a local bar. When they shared a couple of anecdotes about their cruise ship experience, she regretted that she hadn't made time for a real vacation in years.

"I've never been on a cruise like that," she admitted. "When I finished my ROTC commitment, I went straight into private security."

"That's a shame," Kian said. "Between job moves is the best time to blow off steam."

She grinned. He made a good point. "My schedule hasn't meshed with the friends I'd want to go with." Something about taking a cruise by herself seemed sad and pitiful.

"So go alone," Kian suggested. "Make friends on the cruise."

Beside her Lane tensed up. It was there and gone so fast she wasn't sure she'd really felt it at all. "I'll think about it," she said. Friends didn't have to be forever people, although she did envy the tight connection these men shared. Of course, they didn't get this close by hanging out in bars. They'd worked together on challenging operations and trained hard when they weren't putting their lives on the line all across the globe.

"You could always take a new friend," Lane said softly.

The back of his hand slid along the side of her thigh. She thought he was reaching for something in the side pocket of his shorts, except his hand stayed there. The casual contact felt good, the heat of his hand radiating through the thin fabric of her pants.

"Are you volunteering?"

"Depends on the destination." His lightning-quick grin reminded her of their brief encounters on the beach. Because they had an audience? Whatever the reason, it stirred up doubts in her head.

This wasn't a date. They weren't here to decide if they were compatible enough for date two. They barely knew each other and she didn't see much need for that to change. So why did she want to kiss him so badly? Right this instant. The adrenaline of the search had waned. She wasn't tipsy at all. It seemed as if she was getting a second wind. She didn't think that was good news.

"We should get going," Kian's voice cut through her thoughts. "Need to rest up before Hawk calls us back into the action."

"What action?" Waylen grumbled as he slid out of the booth. "All we've been doing is standing around waiting for someone to need a hand." He shoved his hands into his pockets. "Oh." He glanced around before handing over the twenty-two she'd given Drake. "You'll want this back."

"Thanks." Cassie tucked the gun out of sight and then nudged Lane out of the way so she could stand up. "And thanks again for helping with Drake." She gave him a quick, hard hug.

"I was there too," Kian said. "With all my medical expertise."

"And I'm so grateful." She hugged the medic. "You saved his life."

When his friends walked out, Lane frowned at her. "You're grateful, even though your partner might be working against you?"

"If he is, I'll gladly take him down." She sat

down again, tucking the gun into her purse before reaching for her beer. "If he's fooled me all this time, I'll make it right."

"Sorry." Lane sat down next to her, rather than take an open seat on the far side of the table. He angled himself, as if shielding her from view. "I brought you here to relax, not to get you amped up again."

"I'm relaxed." She drained the last of her beer. "And I've had the prescribed one beer."

"You're allowed to have another one." His smile was warm. "I'll be your designated driver."

She didn't need more to drink. She needed to figure out which Lane was the real deal. "No, thanks. It is late and—" She yawned. "See? Sleep should be next on my agenda."

"Fine by me."

They walked out to the Wrangler and the events of the day caught up to her. She ached from head to toe, feeling as if she'd been flattened by a steamroller. When Lane opened the passenger door for her, she hopped in and buckled up. Noticing a piece of paper wedged into the driver's seat, she pulled it out and smoothed the creases.

"Damn." Laugh or cry? She had no idea how to react to another print out of that stupid picture from the beach with the red circle and slash over her face.

"Cassie?" Lane climbed into the car. "Talk to me."

She fought the urge to look around for whoever might be watching for a reaction. "First, promise you won't do or say anything."

"No." That stern tone sent a shiver over her skin. "What's in your hand?"

"Just some trash," she said, a little louder than necessary. "Let's go."

He obliged, starting the engine. "Show me."

She shook her head. "No need. It's the same photo they planted on Drake. You think it's related to whoever tailed us here?"

"Seems likely," Lane replied. "No shame in having lots of enemies, though."

"Gee, thanks." She used her phone to send a text documenting the incident. "Just be careful."

"Always. Alert and careful, that's me."

As he drove, the wind caught in her hair, teasing strands of it loose from her braid. Alert and careful was not how she'd describe the man who'd approached her on the beach. No, that guy had been carefree, in full vacation mode, hunting up someone to be a new friend, to use Kian's phrase. A far cry from the man who'd come to her aid tonight.

She marveled at that. He'd shown up for a stranger and he'd made a difference. Multiple times. With no hesitation, he'd just done the right thing at the right time.

There were layers to Lane Benning. Strangely enough she liked each one more than the last. "Are we being followed?"

"No. I'm not surprised," he added. "They know where you're most likely to go."

Resort or hospital. "True. Should we be unpredictable?"

"Let's save that for tomorrow," he said. "It's late and not the best day to try and find other accommodations."

It occurred to her that the wind must've changed. The ash and sulfur odors weren't nearly as potent now. "Have you visited the Volcanoes National Park?"

He shook his head. "It was on my list. I'm sure they've closed the park until the eruption dies down. What about you?"

"I was out there with the family a couple days ago. Drake too," she remembered. "It's…" She struggled to find the right words. "It's awe-inspiring. A completely foreign landscape." She laughed at herself. "That probably sounds like something out of the brochure."

"Nah. You sound sincere. Like a tourist who enjoyed the experience."

Encouraged, she continued. "The hike was incredible and the views were amazing. I could've stayed up there for days taking pictures of everything from the ocean and sky to the black rocks under our feet. I wasn't alone, obviously, but I felt alone. If that makes any sense."

"Does to me."

"I confess, it freaks me out that we were right there, about forty-eight hours before an eruption." She hadn't let herself think about that. Natural disasters were outside her scope as a protector, of course. Didn't make it any less unsettling when she thought of how close they'd come to danger and tragedy.

"You keep asking me who gains if I'm out of the way."

"And?" he prompted.

"No idea. I'm more like a cog in a wheel. I know I do good work, but I'm hardly irreplaceable."

"Matter of opinion."

She ignored the comment. He had to be teasing her. "I do know countless people and businesses would suffer if Judith Knowles disappeared."

"How so?"

"Billions in government contracts would be left in limbo. She has competent staff and I'm sure everything is documented and organized correctly, but it would be a big mess for a while."

Lane didn't respond and she figured he was considering how that might explain or fit into the mystery she was tangled up in. At the resort, he parked and took her hand as they walked inside. The big question of where she should sleep loomed in her mind. She didn't want to kick him out of his room, but she didn't quite trust herself to be alone with him any longer than necessary.

"I'd love to see the pictures you took the other day," Lane said. "Not tonight, though." At his room, he tapped the keycard and opened the door, keeping her just behind him.

She didn't realize she was braced for the worst until her shoulders unwound. Thankfully, everything was just as they'd left it.

He gave her hand a squeeze. "Yeah, me too." Releasing her, he walked over to the far side of the bed and grabbed a pillow. "I'll take the floor."

"You can't do that."

"Cassie."

"No." She stopped him, suspecting he was ready to argue the wrong point. "I know you want to stick close."

"I did promise your boss I would."

"That's not the problem." She didn't know what to do with her hands so she shoved them into her pockets. "You should take the bed. I can sleep in the chair or on the floor."

He advanced on her. "No can do."

"Why not? Because I'm female?" He shifted and she knew she was right.

"Chivalry. Manners. Whatever you want to call it," he said too casually. "You're taking the bed."

"That's not a valid reason."

His gaze dropped to the pillow in his hands. "You want to share?" He tossed the pillow aside and slowly advanced. "We can be adults about this."

Adults, yes. That's what she wanted to be. A consenting adult sharing a bed with Lane. With each step he took, her pulse seemed to lurch into a higher gear. Some small voice warned her that the next few minutes were fraught with life-changing potential. Consequences could wait. Some risks were worth the fallout.

Right now, the heated promise in Lane's pale blue gaze was too tempting. She licked her lips, anticipating what might come next. What she wanted to happen. A tremor rolled up from her feet, but this time it had nothing to do with the island or its high-achieving volcano. It was as if her body was simmering, ready to boil over at the first touch.

Lane's first touch, to be precise.

She couldn't recall the last time she'd felt this pull, this need that refused to be suppressed or denied. "What is it about you?" She hadn't meant for the words to escape her head. Too late to call them back.

His mouth tilted into a wry smile. "I could say the same."

He was close enough now that his warmth wrapped around her. She barely resisted the urge to burrow into him. She knew if she did, he'd hold her close for as long as she liked. So tempting. She recalled the way he'd prevented her fall during their search for Josie. The power of his hands and arms, the breadth of his chest.

"I really want to kiss you." *Understatement of the year.* She wasn't sure how much longer she could hold herself back.

"Then let's do that." He bent his head, his hand sliding up under her hair.

His breath feathered over her lips and then—finally—his mouth covered hers. Sensations swamped her, one after the other, leaving her breathless and delighted and longing for more.

For as much as he'd give.

Her hands gripped his shoulders and she pulled herself closer. He drew her in until she was pressed against him, chest to thigh. She sighed over the wonder of him, taking the kiss deeper still. His tongue stroked over hers and a heady shiver skipped down her spine. The world fell away to just this, the two of them and all these delicious sensations. Everything about him seemed to ignite something deep and exciting inside her, leaving her breathless and weak and empowered all at once.

He eased back and she gulped in air, staring up at him. "That was… Um, wow."

Somehow, she felt cheated and rewarded all at once. Who knew kisses could be like that? No one in her past had stirred up this fire in her blood with a simple kiss. His palms glided up along her ribs, stopping short of her aching breasts, and slowly back down. His fingers flexed at her waist.

"A big wow." He closed his eyes and took a deep breath. "We should probably hit pause here."

Was that a question? It took her a beat to agree with him. Pausing couldn't be the right move when her body was all-in on whatever pleasure he was willing to explore with her.

"You're right." She pressed up on her toes and kissed a path along his jaw. He skimmed a hand over her hip as she retreated. "You are also irresistible."

"Thanks for noticing."

She laughed, her hands smoothing over his chest.

He stroked her lower lip. "Same goes."

Was it terrible that she wanted him to touch her forever? She should give him space. He'd been the one to mention pausing and she didn't want to be clingy or pushy. She looked to the bed and quickly away. "We could share," she offered.

"Our feelings?"

"Ha." She wasn't ready to go there. Sex was one thing, but whenever she shared more than her body, problems cropped up. A therapist had labeled it "abandonment issues". Oddly enough, naming the problem didn't automatically fix it. Though Cassie had tried, she still found it challenging to trust personal connections enough to really open up with someone. "I meant the bed."

He shook his head. "I don't think so." He ran a hand through his hair and took a step back. "That's mission impossible for me, Cass. You're too tempting."

"Pillows between us?"

He retrieved the pillow he'd grabbed earlier. "I've taken down fortresses," he said. "A pillow is hardly enough of a barrier if the prize is you."

He saw her as a prize?

"Stop that," he grumbled.

"What?" She had no idea what he was talking about.

"That. The look on your face," he circled a finger in the general direction of her face. "Like you don't know how desirable you are."

She really didn't think about it much.

"I'm not rushing this," he stated. "Not tonight. Take the bed."

She recognized an order when she heard one. "Fine."

"Thank you." He kissed her cheek as he passed her to pull an extra blanket down from the closet shelf. "And sleep well. I've got your back."

She knew he was right not to rush whatever was happening here. The moment her head touched the pillow, bone-deep exhaustion weighed her down. Despite the lust swirling in her system, she couldn't fight the weariness. Figuring out what Drake was scared of and who was harassing her would require energy and clear thinking.

Besides, when she and Lane did take the leap and share a bed, she wanted to be doing it for the right reasons. There were already enough regrets to haunt her from this assignment. She didn't want Lane Benning to be one of them.

8

*L*ane knew the moment Cassie woke up because he was already awake. Awake and thinking about that kiss. He'd been staring at the ceiling for at least an hour, wishing he could do something about the erection that wouldn't give up this morning.

He'd been afraid to move and wake her before she was ready. She needed the rest. Worse, he wasn't sure how she might react to his rather obvious arousal. Thank God they weren't sharing the bed. In that scenario, he wouldn't trust *his* self-control.

Last night he'd held her in his arms and everything had felt right. Perfect. She'd been eager and responsive. Remembering the way she pressed against him wasn't helping his current predicament.

If his buddies ever learned he'd turned her down—insisting on sleep over sex—he'd never hear the end of it. Finally, something that cooled his ardor a bit.

None of them wasted time bragging about one conquest or another, so he didn't have cause to be truly worried. Although he'd have to be careful around Harlan. His friend had a way of looking through a man and knowing stuff he shouldn't know.

"You awake?" Cassie's voice, husky from sleep, stirred him up all over again.

"I am." He propped himself up on one elbow. "Rested?"

"Yes." The covers shifted as she stretched. "Thank you." A moment later, she was peering at him over the end of the bed. "Did you get any sleep?"

Her hair tumbled in loose waves around her face, over her shoulders. Wouldn't take much to reach out and wind those silky strands around his fingers. Would take even less to tumble her back, cover her, and make it a morning to remember.

Down boy.

"I slept fine." For about four hours. Enough to take the edge off and recharge. His fingers stroked across hers. Too tempting. He pulled back. They had things to do today.

"I like your tattoo," she said, pointing to his shoulder.

"Thanks." There were times when he forgot

about the compass and the curling wave cutting through the middle of it. His only reminder of home these days. "You want the shower first?"

She sat up on her knees. "No! New rule: whoever sleeps on the floor gets the bathroom first."

"Fine. But avert your eyes," he warned. "I'm not dressed."

He rolled to his feet and felt her gaze on him. As tender and hot as her touch last night. Glancing back, he chuckled. "See something you like?"

"Absolutely everything." She slowly dragged her eyes up to meet his. Something shifted in her expression and he would've given up a limb to know what she was thinking. Since when did he have such an intense need to know a woman inside and out?

"Special," he murmured to himself, walking away from her.

He had to leave the personal queries for later. Had to ignore the sizzling chemistry between them. For now.

Once they got some answers out of Drake, he would reassess. He didn't want to tangle this up and complicate things. He needed her to be confident in him and his abilities. He couldn't risk that she might think his commitment to protect her was predicated on his attraction or hers.

He turned on the shower and immediately stepped under the spray, not caring about the temperature. The colder the better right now.

A couple of minutes later, the door opened a crack and a bolt of anticipation shot through him. Unfortunately, only her voice joined him inside.

"I'm ordering breakfast. Room service," she clarified.

"Great, thanks."

"And, *um…*"

Finished, he turned off the water, waiting before he reached for a towel.

"There's an extra pot of coffee. Claudia called. She says the police are on the way over." Cassie pulled the door closed before he could respond.

Drying off quickly, he wrapped the towel around his waist and walked out of the bathroom. "All yours." He enjoyed the way her eyes went wide, skimming over him from head to toe again. She was the sweetest boost for his ego. Then she rushed by, carrying clean clothes with her.

Too bad he wouldn't get to enjoy the delectable view of her in a towel. Memories of her in the bikini would tide him over until they could make new, intimate memories together. The more she looked at him that way, the more it seemed inevitable.

He straightened the bed and tucked away the extra blanket, making the room more presentable for what he expected would be an official visit. Hopefully, he wouldn't have to deal with the cops by himself.

In less than ten minutes, she emerged looking refreshed and ready for the day. One more thing to admire about her. Her sleeveless shirt, another floral print, showed off her tanned, toned arms. She'd left it untucked over lightweight navy blue pants. He figured it was an outfit that would blend well in the normal course of her role as a protector. Plus, she could hide her weapons, and move freely if a physical response was required. She'd swept back her hair into a smooth knot at the back of her head, leaving the nape of her neck bare. He suddenly wanted to kiss her right there.

"Why are you staring?"

"Check a mirror," he said. "You're breathtaking." He stopped before giving her a full litany of the compliments filling his mind.

Indulging temptation had to wait until after the police visit. Longer, really. He knew how badly she wanted to speak with her partner about the tie to Greenlee and his involvement in the stunt with Josie.

"Thanks." Her cheeks went pink. She tugged at the hem of her shirt. "Do we need a plan for the police? Should we review our story?"

He snagged his phone from the dresser and sent texts to Hawk and Waylen. "I hope not. We don't have anything to hide so that makes it simple. I just want to be caffeinated before they arrive."

"Same." She pressed her fingers against her palms, alternating and stretching her hands. "The message from Claudia didn't give me any cause for real worry. She said my bosses, both lawyers, were working on it from their end."

"We didn't do anything wrong," he reminded her.

"Except leave a body in the rainforest."

"Greenlee started it," Lane reminded her. "And we had a higher purpose to reunite Josie with her family. She's a minor, her safety was the priority."

She caught her lip between her teeth. "Let's hope they see it that way."

He couldn't help it, he closed the distance and laid a soft kiss on her lips. "We did what was necessary." Her hands lifted to his shoulders so he kissed her again. "Besides, we have reliable backup between your people and mine."

She smiled and gave him a squeeze. "Reliable and willing to post bail."

"That too." He held her, simply enjoying the closeness, glad to see the shadows under her eyes had faded overnight.

Lane got his caffeine wish as room service arrived first. He and Cassie had fueled up and were lingering over coffee when the police knocked on the door. He noticed the shift in her demeanor. She straightened her shoulders, her expression serious as she braced for the official conversation.

At that moment, she looked like the woman who had called Hawk for help. Competent, in control, utterly unflappable. If he hadn't seen it for himself, he wouldn't believe anyone who claimed she knew how to relax and unwind.

Apparently, her professional approach was exactly what the two responding officers needed to see. Lane poured coffee and the interview was brief and polite, if not particularly friendly. Better still, no one ended up in handcuffs or in the back of a patrol car. The officers did share their condolences on Josie's ordeal, along with news that Greenlee's body had been recovered and moved to the morgue.

The four of them visited Cassie's room where the officers took a statement about the break in there, calling in a forensics team to gather any evidence. They warned her the laptop was likely gone for good, despite the tracking device. Before leaving the resort, they urged both Lane and Cassie to stay in town and—in case it came up—not to leave the scene of another crime.

Naturally, Lane and Cassie eagerly agreed to those terms.

When they were alone again in his room, she threw herself at him, hugging him tightly. "Thank you! I would've broken apart without your support."

He doubted that. He held her at arm's length, his hands gentle on her shoulders. "What are you talking about? You were a rock."

She shook her head. "I was sweating bullets."

"Well, it didn't show."

She swore, stepping out of his reach. "I forgot to ask them about Drake. I don't want to run into them at the hospital."

"If we do, it only proves you're invested in your partner's well-being. Might actually work in our favor," he added. "They only told us to stay in town. We're not limited to the resort."

"Good point." She shook out her hands. "I was sure they'd haul us in for leaving the body."

He'd been concerned too and was glad to put the possibility behind him. Being so close to her tested his self-control, and he tucked his hands into his pockets.

All he could think of was her. Her kiss, her touch. Her exuberant hugs soothed something deep in his chest. Something he hadn't known was off. It was strange, for all his wanderlust since retiring, he never expected another *person* to be part of the solution as he searched for contentment. Whatever this connection was between them, he appreciated being dropped into her life. Getting to know her revealed parts of himself he needed to better understand.

"Hey." She smoothed a hand up and down his arm. "You okay?"

He grinned at her. "Better than okay." As he watched, the concern in her eyes eased. "Ready to head over to the hospital?"

"Sure." She nodded. "Just let me tell my bosses we're in the clear with the local police."

He updated Hawk and got back a message that his buddies were deployed to various locations around the island today. He understood it was a warning that he was on his own and backup might not be as readily available.

Just one more reason to avoid trouble today.

Outside, as they left the resort, the skies overhead were a stunning blue. "Winds must've changed," he said. "Hard to believe the crisis they're coping with on the other side of the island."

Cassie agreed. "As long as the ground stays firm and quiet today, I'm a happy girl."

"Let me guess, no earthquakes in Iowa either."

"As if you didn't know that." She nudged his shoulder. "Did you have to deal with earthquakes growing up in California?"

He shot her a look. "How'd you come to that conclusion?"

"You're kidding." She flicked a hand at him. "The SoCal-surf's-up vibe is all over you."

"Nah. That's retirement from a demanding career," he hedged. "I'm not even sure I remember where I grew up."

"You remember," she accused lightly. "When was the last time you were home?"

He shifted in the seat, not exactly eager to have this conversation. "When my mom died," he said. "After she died, to be precise." Precision had been important in his career, not so much in his personal life. Something about Cassie made him want to try and be clear.

"I was deployed when she passed." Hearing a sympathetic noise from Cassie, he tried to roll right past it. "We were close. Never knew my dad, though my grandparents told me I didn't miss much. And you were right about SoCal. I grew up in Malibu. I grew up surfing and then I joined the Navy. I'm a walking stereotype."

"Hardly."

Though she probably considered it a compliment, he wasn't letting her off the hook. "You're the one who wouldn't talk to me because you thought I was a player."

"Aren't you?"

At the stop light, he caught her hand, bringing it to his lips. "Guilty as charged. Before you."

The stern expression on her face melted and the amusement sparkling in her eyes enchanted him. He probably deserved her doubts, considering how persistent he'd been when they'd been strangers on the beach.

"Let me guess." He released her as the light changed. "Claudia spilled all my secrets?"

"Just the basic background intel. She's a stickler for privacy. Not like she listed your military service awards or anything."

A chill washed over him. Yes, he'd earned a few commendations along the way, but those came at a price. Some of them would remain classified for decades to come. "She didn't."

Cassie patted his thigh. "No, she did not." She pulled her hand back, lacing her fingers together in her lap. "My short stint in the Army was a walk in the park compared to your career as a SEAL. I wouldn't presume to understand the sacrifices you made."

He turned into the hospital parking lot. Once he'd found a space and cut the engine, she swiveled in her seat. Taking his hands in hers, she said, "I'm sorry you missed your mom's service."

"Cassie, it was ten years ago." He was over it. She'd been sick, he'd been there as much as possible, though it didn't change the outcome. The cancer had been aggressive. His mom understood, absolving him of any hint of neglect. She'd been that proud of the man he'd become and how he'd chosen to serve his country.

Suddenly, his eyes burned and his throat felt tight. He looked to the sky. Where was an ash cloud to take the blame when he needed one?

"Parents matter, whether we want them to or not," Cassie said. "Mine died when I was a kid. The service was awful. Didn't do anything to capture or honor what I loved most about my mom and dad."

"How old were you?" he asked.

"Ten. Too young to give any input in the service. The eulogy felt so distant, as if they were talking about strangers. Maybe because I was too young." She nipped at her lip. "Anyway, I went straight from the post-service dinner at the church to my uncle's farm. There wasn't much choice. Not for any of us. And farm chores were better than foster care, so I've been told."

"You lost everything at once," he said, incredulous.

Temper simmered for the grieving child she'd been. People made the dumbest decisions. No kid should have to be uprooted like that. Sure, she was sitting here looking beautiful and well-adjusted, but that must've sucked big time. He admired her more knowing that she'd overcome, adapted, and made choices that clearly suited her.

"That's right." She nodded. "Home, school, and friends. Gone within a week." She took a deep breath. "My point is that there were things that were handled poorly. Those were seriously dark days for me. And things I had to reframe and restructure for myself when I was old enough to do so. Did you ever consider doing that? Didn't anyone suggest it?"

Focused on her and her past, he had no idea what she was talking about. "What do you mean?"

"You could have your own memorial service for your mom. Well, for you, really."

He'd never met anyone as kind as Cassie. She seemed to lead with her heart, no matter the situation. It was such a risky approach to life, one he wasn't nearly as comfortable with. Somehow she managed it without compromising the integrity of the job.

He recognized her as someone to learn from. Here he was, a retired SEAL without a clear next step, though he was sure there was some purpose hovering near the horizon, waiting for him to find it. An opportunity to use the skills he'd honed during his service.

"They offered to delay the service," he said. "Didn't work for me. They needed to grieve. I have a recording. It was fine. Big turnout." He sniffled. "She would've gotten a kick out of the things her friends shared."

"What about you?" Cassie pressed.

There it was again, that big heart leading the way. But it made him smile. "I went to the beach where she taught me to surf," he said. "She lived and breathed the surf's-up vibe you pinned on me."

"No wonder you carry it with so much pride," she said softly. "It's to honor her. The tattoo is for her, right?"

"Yes. Did that way before she got sick." He could stop, keep the rest to himself, but that didn't feel right. "I went out early with the guys." Harlan, Raider, Waylen, and Kian wouldn't let him go alone. "I felt her out there with me. In the quiet waiting, and beside me on the waves. I scattered her ashes in the ocean."

It had been the best he could do for his mom, for himself.

Somehow, sharing the story with Cassie, he felt better about all of it. Settled and calm, where there used to be a lingering pinch of guilt.

"Thanks," he said. "For listening. I didn't know I needed to talk about it."

Her smile warmed him straight through. "What are friends for?"

He leaned over and kissed her, taking his time and making it clear he wouldn't be dropped in the friend zone.

Sitting back, he considered the demonstration a success based on the dazzled look in her eyes. "Friends are good for all kinds of things," he said, tucking a loose strand of hair behind her ear. "Let's go figure out why your partner was talking to the enemy."

9

*T*alking to the enemy.

The phrase echoed in Cassie's mind as she and Lane made their way up to Drake's room. As much as she wanted to deny it, the facts backed up the words. Her partner had been seen chatting up Greenlee. Mere hours before Josie went missing. And last night he'd been terrified that Greenlee was coming to kill him.

"Is that black and white outlook a permanent thing?" she asked Lane when they stepped out of the elevator on Drake's floor.

He took her hand, as if they walked together like this all the time. "Plenty of gray areas in the world."

"I agree. But you called Greenlee the enemy."

Lane pulled up short, abruptly turning down a

different hallway. He pressed a finger to his lips when she started to ask questions.

She hushed, wondering what had spooked him.

"Police," he whispered. "Plainclothes. Feds, maybe."

That was a new development and the last thing she'd expected. "You're sure?"

He nodded. Still holding her hand, he kept moving, leading her further from Drake's room. She didn't want to get caught up in another legal issue, but she wasn't leaving this hospital without talking to her partner.

They reached a sunny room with big windows all the way across one wall with a jaw-dropping view. Chairs were clustered in small groups throughout the long room along with a few tables. A shelving unit on the far wall held books and games and there was a table with a checkerboard set up and another with an unfinished puzzle.

"Greenlee took aim and fired on us. In my book that makes him an enemy," Lane said.

Seemed rude to argue with that logic while his fingers circled the faint burn on her upper arm from the bullet that had nearly hit her.

Lane's assessment put Greenlee in the bad-guy column regardless of whether or not he was still tied to Welker Specialists. She needed to keep an open mind. It would be silly to underestimate any leads Drake might provide.

"Good point," she allowed.

It was never smart to assume full understanding of a problem. In this instance, she didn't have a clear motive for the ambush. Neither did the agency. Which was why she needed to talk to her partner.

Continuing on through the bright lounge, she realized they were circling around and would approach Drake's room from the opposite end of the hallway. "Why are we sneaking around? We have every right to be here."

"True. But something feels off. I expected to see the same cops who visited us. I want to know who these guys are and why they posted a guard to watch the elevator. If we can get close enough, maybe we'll overhear something helpful before we're noticed."

She was on board for more intel. Mentally, she crossed her fingers that his idea would work. Lane peered around the corner, then strolled forward. The guard in front of Drake's room had his back to them, completely focused on the activity near the elevator.

The ward was bustling and, compared to last night, it was as if someone had cranked up the volume to ten. Between the many voices and machines, it would be impossible to eavesdrop.

Lane seemed to come to the same conclusion. "Plan B?"

"If that means walking right in like we own the place, let's go."

He smiled. "Great minds think alike."

Giving her hand a squeeze, he released her. She didn't have time to miss his touch as he placed that same hand at the small of her back. This wasn't normal for her. Most of the time, she craved more personal space, not less. On the rare times she dated, she knew she came across as standoffish. At work, she wouldn't tolerate this contact at all, unless an undercover op demanded the appearance of intimacy. In fact, she couldn't imagine a situation where she wouldn't shy away from close contact. Yet here she was, wondering what it was about Lane that made her want to snuggle up and stay there.

Further analysis had to wait. Their approach had drawn attention. Both the guard outside the door and a man just inside Drake's room had spotted them.

The man inside stepped out, pulling the door closed behind him. He was big and broad with long dark hair and island tribal tattoos on his forearms. "No visitors."

"I'm his sister," Cassie said, but the fib didn't work this morning.

"We know better, ma'am." He glared at Lane. "You got something to add?"

"Drake's a good friend. Is he in some kind of legal trouble?" Lane queried, acting concerned and innocent. Beside her, he seemed utterly relaxed. "If so, shouldn't he have a lawyer present?"

"This isn't your business."

"Oh, that sounds like a 'yes' to me." She pulled her phone from her pocket. "I know who to call."

She was mostly bluffing. The Guardian Agency was surely aware of whatever was going on. But the big guy shifted on his feet. "Just be patient. You can talk to him when we're done."

She wanted to get inside that room. Now, not later. She was positive Lane wanted the same thing. "Drake shouldn't be alone." She spoke loudly, hoping Drake would hear her.

The big man glared down at her, looming closer. "When. We're. Done."

Lane moved and Cassie suddenly found herself tucked at his back. "You don't want to threaten her," he warned. His body was primed and ready for a fight. There was nothing laid back or easy-going about him now.

For a moment, she worried he would start something, but she should've known better. Lane had proven time and again that he was steady when it mattered most.

The big guy withdrew, refusing to look at them, but continued standing firmly in their path. By some tacit agreement, she and Lane retreated to the opposite side of the hall, staying out of the way, while remaining close to Drake's room. Trusting

Lane to keep watch, she messaged Claudia about this latest wrinkle.

She received an immediate assurance that the interview was above board and Swann and Gamble were aware of the situation. Tilting her screen to share the news with Lane, his eyebrows furrowed. His perplexed expression mirrored her own feelings.

Minutes ticked by, each one feeling like hours, before the door finally swung open. The big guard moved with surprising quickness to clear the path for a man and woman to exit. She immediately agreed with Lane's assessment about plainclothes, possibly federal, officers. Dressed in loose linen shirts and khakis, there was no way to determine what law enforcement agency they represented. That didn't give her any comfort as the team of four marched away.

"Our turn," she said, taking Lane's hand and crossing the hall.

When she saw Drake, tears filled her eyes. He looked worse today instead of better. Pale under the bruises, she was sure the meeting hadn't helped matters. Her heart swelled. This man was her partner. Her friend. If he'd made mistakes, she'd deal with the fallout. She wouldn't write him off until she had a damn good reason.

And proof. Acres of proof.

"You weren't ready for that, were you?" she

asked from the foot of the bed. After last night's close call, she wouldn't move closer.

"Go away, Cass." He rolled to his side, letting out a pained groan. "Stay out of this."

"I will," she promised. Just as soon as she understood what "this" was. "How about you take a nap? We'll keep watch for you."

"You're relentless," Drake grumbled without looking at her.

She didn't need to make eye contact to see that something was taking a toll on him. Shame or guilt, she wanted to be sure. "Thanks."

"Wasn't a compliment."

"It is if I want it to be." She glanced back over her shoulder and found Lane propping up the door. She wasn't sure Drake realized she wasn't here alone. "Go to sleep. I won't let anyone disturb you."

"Stop being nice to me. This isn't your problem anymore."

That raised red flags, but she didn't reply, determined to match his stubbornness. Moving around the bed, she sat down in the chair, stifling the cringe over his battered face. He glared at her through swollen eyes. "Why would Greenlee want you dead?"

"Leave." He sounded exhausted. "Please."

At the door, Lane tapped his wrist.

She'd much rather give Drake time to recuperate. "Let me help you. What did the feds want?"

He cleared his throat. "You don't know——"

"Give me some credit, Drake." She leaned forward, bracing her elbows on her knees. "You like the Knowles. You wouldn't betray me. And you would never—*never*—put Josie, or any other kid, in danger. Loop me in. What did they want?"

"The little things." He adjusted the pillow under his cheek. "They weren't random."

Not a direct answer. They'd both been irritated with those incidents that made them look like below-average bodyguards. She waited through his spate of coughing. Breathing seemed to pain him. "Broken ribs?"

He nodded. With an effort, he pressed the button that elevated his head. She moved to help with the pillow this time. Spotting Lane at the door, Drake swore.

"You don't have the energy to be annoyed with anyone. Not even yourself," she said. "Did you forget Lane saved your life?"

"I remember."

"Good." She took pity on him. "If you suspected Greenlee, why didn't you tell me?"

"The association is embarrassing," he said. "Stupid mistake years ago." He shifted with an effort. "Guardian Agency gave me a second chance."

"They're good at that." She smiled down at her friend. "Tell me the rest."

147

"There was never any proof, Cass. I noticed him and assumed the worst."

"Rightly so," Lane interjected. He pointed to the clock on the wall. "We're running out of time. The nurse will give us the boot when she comes around again."

Drake grunted. "Short version." He struggled through another cautious breath. "I tried to get Greenlee to confide in me and it backfired. My plan all along was to tell you and the bosses, as soon as we reached Hawaii."

"What changed your mind?" she asked.

"Welker Specialists. I didn't know Greenlee was with them. You have to believe me." His gaze pleaded for understanding. Forgiveness. "They want the Knowles job."

"Why?"

"I don't know," he admitted. "When Greenlee showed up here, I knew I'd waited too long. He had a plan, but he didn't tell me what it was. Just that he'd pin the blame on us, and then Welker would swoop in to save the day."

Lane gripped the panel at the end of the bed. "You agreed to let them terrorize Josie?"

She didn't appreciate the interruption, though she could hardly fault him for demanding an answer to the question that was at the forefront of her mind.

"Hell, no." Drake shook his head. "No. I had no idea he'd do that."

"It's okay." Cassie rested a hand on his shoulder. "I believe you."

"Seriously?" Lane gaped at her. "I don't believe a word of this." He glared at Drake. "That girl barely got away from Greenlee and his pals. They wanted you dead, I assume to guarantee your silence. They tried to kill Cassie. You *will* keep talking. You owe her that much."

Was this some good cop, bad cop routine? This was no way to treat her partner, a man she'd relied on for months. He'd never let her down. Until yesterday. She expected the feds had bullied him earlier and she didn't want to pile on.

"Maybe you should wait in the hall," she suggested to Lane.

He shook his head, his lips in a hard line. "I'm good right here." He folded his arms over his chest.

"It doesn't matter." Drake scrubbed at his face. "You rescued Josie and the family is safe. Greenlee can't cause more trouble. The feds are on it now."

"Why?" Cassie and Lane demanded at the same time.

Drake sputtered, his gaze darting from her to Lane and back again. "I don't know. Not all of it. They must've been watching Welker for a while. That's all I got out of their visit. Let them do their thing."

"Give me something, Drake." She couldn't expect him to be at his best when he was struggling to recover, but she needed more information. Details to explain the ambush and the break in at her room. "Who was Greenlee working with? I'll talk to Gamble and Swann for you."

"Already talked with them." Tears leaked from Drake's eyes. "Nurse brought in a phone before the feds showed up. I told them you had no idea what I was trying to accomplish."

She fumed, struggling to hide her reaction. This was not how it was supposed to work. She was the lead—he should've brought his suspicions to her. Well, she had one likely answer. Swann had relieved her from the Knowles assignment because she'd been too ignorant to figure out that her partner was up to something.

"Cassie, you need to go."

Fine. "We're leaving." She couldn't look at him.

"Watch your back," Drake said.

She stalked out of the room.

"You too." Lane said the words she couldn't.

He caught up with her at the elevator. She jabbed the call button repeatedly. "That's done then," she muttered. "Between the feds and our bosses, Drake has all the protection he needs."

"All right." Lane tucked his hands in his pockets. "And you have me. No one has to split focus."

"Right," she replied through gritted teeth. She

should be happier about Lane's commitment to her safety. She *was*. Lane was definitely on her side. He had no skin in the game. "Thank you."

She heard him chuckle and whipped around. "You're laughing?"

"Only because you're so pissed." He brushed his knuckles across her cheek. "Looks good on you."

"We didn't learn anything useful."

"I disagree. Your partner—"

"Former partner." She'd never work with Drake again. Her trust in him had been shattered. "He should have come to me."

Her chest ached, as if a vine was cinching her ribcage, making it harder and harder to breathe. This was not the time or place to have her abandonment issues rearing up and trashing her concentration. Recognizing the escalating sensation only made matters worse. In therapy, she'd been told that understanding where it was coming from was a healthy step forward and gave her room to cope and grow.

This didn't feel like growth. Felt more like hell. Her parents had been jerked out of her life by chance, not choice. Drake had made bad choices that severed a bond she valued. Tears she couldn't let fall stung her eyes. Her self-control was disintegrating.

"He was right beside me the whole time." She wanted to pummel something. Someone. Except

Greenlee had beat her to it and the medical team would frown on her adding to Drake's injuries. "I look like an idiot."

"No, you don't." Lane drew her into a hug. "Breathe," he urged. "You're furious. It'll fade."

She wasn't so sure about that, even as she welcomed the comfort Lane offered. A little voice in her head wondered how long he'd stick around. Why would he stick at all? She couldn't expect him to shadow her forever. She didn't even want that.

"When it fades," Lane continued, "you'll realize that the feds are using your partner to get a line on Welker."

She jerked away, her gaze narrowing as she studied him. "You knew who I was talking about last night."

He raised his hands in surrender. "I didn't. Waylen sent me some intel this morning."

"Great." She sagged back against the elevator wall. "So I guess that leaves me in Hawaii without a job."

"I can teach you how to vacation like it's your job," he offered.

"Funny." They exited the elevator and aimed for the parking lot.

"I'm not joking." He stepped closer, his palm hovering at her low back. "I've had months to perfect my process."

His lighthearted tone didn't match the sudden uptick in tension. "What's wrong?"

"Not sure yet."

His jaw was tight. "Are you creating an excuse to touch me?"

"Never." He gave a small shake of his head and his mouth twitched, but his attention was elsewhere. "Greenlee and Drake had some kind of history the feds want to use," he said. "Until someone explains that threatening photo of you, I won't rest easy."

Crap. She was off her game. She'd forgotten about the photo and the stolen laptop. "We should—"

An explosion cut her off. She turned toward the sound and saw a dark plume of smoke rising from what had been a trash can. She started forward, her natural instinct to help, but Lane shoved her down between two parked cars. She landed hard, the pavement biting into her hands and knees.

"Run!"

She stared back at Lane and held her ground, though he frantically waved her off.

Even if she could force herself to leave him, where did he think she'd go?

10

*L*ane swore. He'd sensed something was off and he'd been right. The weapons were locked in the car and with people running around, he couldn't see the real threat. Now, Cassie wasn't cooperating. It was his job to protect her. She needed to get away from this scene, ASAP.

It looked like the explosion was little more than a big smoke bomb. Clearly a distraction tactic. But why? To give one person another chance to kill her? Or were they up against a team ambush this time?

Damn it.

He crouched behind a tire. Further down the same aisle, Cassie did the same. "Go!" He kept his voice low.

She shook her head and mouthed "Where?"

Away from danger. He shook off his irritation that she'd ignore the obvious answer. What did he expect? She was a trained bodyguard. Her career was built around protecting people. When the explosion sounded, she'd lunged in that direction and his heart had stopped.

He wasn't the only person who knew that would be her automatic response. Couldn't be. Anyone observing Cassie at work would see that immediately.

Waylen's latest message, with more background on Welker Specialists, hadn't been any comfort at all. They were the kind of security group that did just enough work on the right side of the law to claim they were respectable in the right circles. Lane could read between the lines. Waylen mentioned rumors of ops that blew past any legal boundaries and general common sense. Welker conducted old fashioned mercenary jobs that kept the company well-funded. On those jobs, they had a reputation for the best equipment, plenty of personnel, and being as slippery as Teflon. No complaints or formal charges would stick to the company.

Now, it seemed, Welker had targeted Cassie. But why?

Answers would wait. Right now, he had to get her out of here. To where? He had no idea. He added that to the growing pile of questions he'd answer later.

Ignoring the shouting going on closer to the explosion, Lane dropped to his stomach. He searched for any movement under the nearby vehicles. There were a few civilians moving around, based on the footwear he could see. Had he overreacted?

First time for everything. Although he felt mission ready, he *was* retired. No training in months meant his instincts could be off. If he had made a mistake here, he didn't care. Cassie's safety was more important than his pride.

They were only a few rows from where he'd parked. If he could get to the Jeep, he'd have access to the weapons and a radio. Being able to defend her and call for backup would make him feel a whole lot better.

He signaled Cassie to wait, then belly-crawled under the truck sheltering him to get a better view of the scene. Alone in the row, he stood up slowly, until he could peer over the edge of the truck bed.

People were still scrambling away from the smoke. He shook his head. No one on this island needed another breathing hazard. When he caught up with the responsible party, he'd gladly break a nose or a jaw for that offense alone.

In the reflection from the side mirror, he caught movement behind him. Not a tourist. The tight t-shirt, bulging muscles, and purposeful stride were a dead giveaway. And that was before Lane spotted the gun. Ducking down low, once more, he hurried back toward Cassie.

"You waited," he said, pressed flat on his belly.

She rolled her eyes. "How many?"

"Only saw one man." Though he doubted the guy was out here alone. "Someone with delusions of becoming The Rock is searching the parking lot. Gun drawn," he added.

"Not a cop?"

"Nope." A cop wouldn't be out here alone. He'd be mic'd up and coordinating with hospital security. He tipped his head. "We need to move. Low and quick." At her nod, he hesitated. "We stay together," he added, just in case she needed the reminder. He had to get her out of here before the police could set up a perimeter. Playing chicken with armed men wasn't his idea of vacation fun.

If the situation was reversed, Lane would put eyes on the target's vehicle. And after missing their shot last night, he suspected Cassie's enemy would be more deliberate and diligent today. With that in mind, he guided her past their car, hoping to get a glimpse of the person serving as the spotter.

With Cassie pressed up close to his hip, he said, "Go to the car." He handed her the keys, making a note of the fresh scrapes on her hands. He'd been too rough back there. He owed her an apology as soon as they were safe. "Back out and drive toward the exit. I'll meet you at the end of the aisle."

Thankfully, she nodded, but before he could move, she gripped his shirt and hauled him close.

The kiss she planted on him was fast, hard, and sexy as hell. "Be smart," she said, giving him a little shake.

"You too," he murmured, but she was already on the move.

He scurried in the opposite direction, passing several cars before popping to his feet. He wanted to draw their attention so Cassie had a chance to get out of range. The lack of immediate reaction gave him a second to doubt his plan, but he didn't pause. Had to stay the course.

At last the reaction came, if a beat slower than he'd hoped. Behind him, someone whistled. Probably The Rock-wannabe. More importantly, the signal drew a reaction from the spotter.

Lane smiled to himself. He'd guessed right and was practically on top of the spotter.

Male, younger than expected. Or maybe Lane was just getting older. Regardless, the guy wore a shirt with the Welker logo on the sleeve.

What a newbie. Poor sap.

That was the extent of Lane's sympathy. He attacked, swift and sure, pulling the man over the edge of the truck bed where he'd been hiding out and watching the parking lot. One quick punch and the guy was out. Lane grabbed his wallet and gun as Cassie drove up.

"Perfect timing." He grinned at her. "I'm driving."

She moved to the passenger seat and buckled up. He dropped the wallet and gun in her lap and drove as quickly as he dared away from the scene.

"Police response seems slow," Cassie said, tucking the gun in the glove box.

"They're in the middle of a bigger crisis," he reminded her. If he didn't know it was impossible, he'd think Welker timed their stunt to coincide with the volcano. But this eruption had surprised everyone, including the experts. As much as he hated to give the enemy any credit, they were currently making the most of the unexpected distraction.

"Anything helpful in the wallet?"

"Just the basics. Some cash, a couple of credit cards. No hotel key. The driver's license is from Kansas, assuming it's real. I'm sending the info up the line. Hang on." She grabbed her cell phone.

"What is it?"

"This guy from Kansas." Another pause. "Yeah. That's him in the picture Mandy took at the resort."

"The nanny?" He was too distracted to remember names.

"Yes. So he had to be in on the kidnapping with Greenlee." She muttered a dire promise to make the man pay. "Claudia will sort it out."

"Hope she's quick. Ask her to inform Hawk too."

"Done," Cassie said after a minute.

"Toss the wallet," he said. "We'll turn over the gun to the cops at the first opportunity."

"Okay."

A few minutes later, Lane nearly groaned. "Does Claudia monitor your location?"

"Yes, why?"

"They're tailing us again," he reported.

She swiveled around, glaring hard at the pickup truck a few cars back. "Back to the bar?"

"Doubt that will work for us today." It was one thing to use that hard curve in the dark. Bright sunlight wouldn't be nearly as effective. Amid a squeal of brakes and blaring car horns, the pickup truck made a move to get around another car, closing the distance between them.

"I don't want to do this here," Lane said, mostly to himself.

The resort was close but he dismissed the option as too predictable. These guys already knew how to find Cassie there.

At the next traffic signal, he changed lanes and turned down a street that would hopefully take him inland, away from the more populated resort area. He didn't know exactly where he was headed, only that he had to lose the tail without injuring any bystanders or drawing the attention and ire of local law enforcement. Based on the erratic driving behind him, it didn't appear that Welker had the same aversion to unwanted consequences.

"What about the ranch?" Cassie asked, her gaze on the side mirror.

"Hawk's wife is pregnant," he said. He wouldn't drag his mess to their doorstep, although he had every confidence Hawk could protect the ranch, his family, and anyone else who might need it. Working together, he believed they could hold their own against the thugs behind them.

"If something happens to me, you should go there. To the ranch, I mean."

She glanced at him. Riding sideways in the seat, she kept her eye on the truck barreling closer. "If something happens to you, I'll be with you. Helping."

"No." An unsettling flare of panic lanced through his chest. He reached out, found her hand and gripped it hard. "Your boss trusted me with your protection. Promise me, Cass. If this goes sideways, you find Hawk."

"I'm not without resources and skills," she reminded him sharply. "We've got this. We just need to get a step ahead of them."

He agreed with her logic, though it was easier said than done at the moment. The pickup truck was gaining. If they made it to the open road, all bets were off. The Wrangler was durable, but the truck had more power. "Let your researchers worry about that," he said. "I need you to find us a place to shake off this guy."

"On it." Phone in hand, she pulled up a local map. "Take the next left."

He did, just as the signal turned yellow. The squealing of tires told him the pickup had followed.

"Left again."

He had to fight his instincts and trust her. She had the map and as much desire to get clear of this mess as he did. He took the turn.

"Second right."

"They're still behind us."

"I'm aware," she said, eyes on her phone. "Take the turn and gun it. Road is clear."

Glancing over, he realized she wasn't using a standard navigation app. Someone else was feeding her the directions in real time. He took the turn, gunned the engine and gained precious distance on the straight, deserted roadway between two warehouses. Checking the rear view, he saw the truck fishtail and clip a garbage bin. The harsh sounds of crunching and scraping metal bounced between the corrugated buildings.

"Stay to the right, toward the trees."

Obediently, he followed her advice through two more intersections as pavement faded to a blackened road that withered to little more than a rutted track leading into a dense green forest. Thanks to a quick cloud burst, his tires didn't kick up any dust to give away their location.

"Don't tell me your Claudia can summon a rain cloud on demand."

She swiveled in her seat, facing forward again. "I wouldn't put it past her."

He kept going, slower now, picking his way along and ready to go off road if the pickup found them.

"No sign of them since the alley," Cassie said.

He found a likely spot and tucked the Wrangler back into the trees, cutting the engine so he could better hear the approach of another vehicle or person. Since the old Jeep didn't have a roof, their clothing was soaked through from the rain. If they'd been anywhere else, they might be chilled. Not here. One more reason to love Hawaii.

They waited in an easy silence for several minutes. At last, he was confident they were clear. "You okay?" he asked.

"I am." She plucked her shirt from her skin, trying to dry it out. "Thanks to you."

"Team effort, all the way." Without her directions, they might still be in a populated area, doing their best to avoid disaster. He rubbed a hand over his head, brushing the water from his short hair. "Gotta say, I worked plenty of missions in messy conditions. Training too. That was the nicest rain ever."

"It's a new experience," she agreed. Reaching back, she pulled the tie from her hair, combed her fingers through the wet locks and wound it into a neat knot once more. "Thanks for getting me out of trouble. Again."

"My pleasure," he said sincerely. Despite understanding the demands of her job and her expertise, he liked being the person watching her back. One of them anyway. "You have friends with interesting access."

She nodded. "I do indeed. As a rule, we don't talk about how our researchers get their intel."

He laughed. "I sure don't want to be on Claudia's bad side."

Her lips tilted and she shook her head. "Drives me nuts that companies like Welker give private security a bad name."

"They give mercenaries a bad name." He climbed out of the car, giving the seat and the rest of him time to dry out. "Lucky for us, the team they sent sucks. The spotter was wearing a company shirt."

Her brow pinched. "Put that way, maybe I should be offended."

He looked over and caught her grinning. No way. *This* made her smile? She couldn't really be so relaxed after all of that. His heart felt heavy inside his chest. What if the truck had stayed on them, or worse, started firing at her?

"This is what? The third direct attempt on your life?"

"Maybe the second." She frowned at him.

"I call bullshit." His hands curled around the windowless door of the rugged little vehicle. The situation, the danger to her, was getting out of hand. "Don't blow this off or underestimate the risks. Those annoying incidents have escalated. Twice in less than twenty-four hours Welker personnel have pointed guns at *you*. I bet there were things in D.C. you didn't even notice."

"Watch yourself, Lane."

He paused, heard his words the way she must have. "That wasn't an insult, just a fact. You were focused on preventing any threat to *the family*. At some point, your partner started working a different agenda."

She was quiet for several minutes. Damn, he'd messed up again. He tried to sort out the best course of action to recover from yet another miscommunication. He willed her to look at him, but she was on her phone. She needed to hear his concerns and take them seriously. They could *not* keep allowing Welker to take pot shots at her. There was a reason she was being targeted. A reason her laptop was stolen. Someone needed to figure that out while he kept her safe.

Aside from scouting, mission intel hadn't been his job. He'd relied on others, then and now. Her team should be working on this, on learning *why* she was in danger. Either they weren't as good as she claimed, or they had other priorities.

Lane gritted his teeth. *His* top priority was her. He was starting to think it would always be her. Shoving aside wispy ideas of the future, he pulled out his phone and sent a message to Waylen asking for any help he had time to provide.

"At no time in D.C. did we find ourselves on the wrong end of a lethal weapon," she said, breaking the silence at last.

Was that significant? It might be. "If I find out the feds are using you as bait, I'll…" He shut his mouth before he revealed too much. He was invested. More than that. He was attached. Hell, he'd barely learned her name and yet she already meant the world to him.

Maybe it was crazy to care so deeply for her. Not that outside opinions would sway him. He'd learned to accept life as it came—the good and the bad.

Cassie was good. Meeting her was a gift. It was that simple for him.

And he wouldn't let her down. He scrubbed a hand over his face and turned away, leaning back against the closed door. The vehicle shifted as she climbed out and came to stand in front of him.

"Thank you for caring," she began. "I'm not nearly as dim or helpless as you seem to think."

"That's a wildly inaccurate interpretation." She

was one of the brightest, most capable people he'd met—and he'd served with the best in the world. He opened his mouth to give her those words and she shushed him.

Pressing her body close, she looped her arms around his neck. "Just kiss me."

He obliged, letting his mouth and hands tell her the things he didn't dare say. Not yet. Maybe not ever, if she booted him out of her life. He wanted her today and tomorrow. He wanted her for as long as she'd have him. His thoughts, his heart had never run off in this direction. It should scare him. Instead he was eager, ready to race headlong into these previously unexplored emotions.

His hands gripped her waist, slid lower over the curve of her hips. The woman was a dream come true in his arms. Better than anything he'd antici- pated the first day he'd spotted her on the beach. He swore and, hating himself for breaking the mood, dragged himself away from her sweet mouth.

"The picture," he said.

She stared up at him, eyes wide and dazed. "What?"

"The one they sent with your face circled. I know where it was taken. The angle," he clarified. He had her full attention now, that sweet lust replaced by intense focus. He looked forward to being able to rekindle that incomparable desire as soon as possible.

She shifted away from him. "Clearly, my kissing skills need work."

"Not true." He brought her close again and smoothed a hand over her hip. "This reminded me."

"My backside reminded you of the photo?"

He looked to the heavens and saw only the green canopy. "I am normally a much better communicator."

"*Mm-hm.* Keep talking. About the photo."

Her hands were soft and warm on his chest. It was a wonder that his damp shirt wasn't giving off steam.

"Do you still have that picture on your phone?"

"Of course." She handed him the device. "Claudia said the metadata confirmed the location."

He glanced down at the awful picture filling the screen and had to pause for a measured breath. Maybe he'd learn that Greenlee had taken it and doctored the image and the silver lining would be that he didn't need to kill anyone else. Though he would never shy away from that task if it kept Cassie safe.

"I'm sure it did." He pinched and zoomed in on the picture as much as possible, growing more confident in his theory. "The water is behind you, meaning the photographer was in the resort."

"I'm sure Claudia has thought of this. Or another tech expert at the agency figured it out."

"Right. But I know *exactly* where the bastard had to be standing. He's above the beach."

"So any number of rooms."

"No. Only one place would give him this angle." He tapped the side of her phone, recalling that morning. Just a few days ago, before he knew her or how he'd feel. Shocking how fast life could change. "You were walking back from the waterfall end of the lagoon."

"To see the turtles. They're beautiful."

He'd gone snorkeling in that lagoon for the same reason. "I get it." Was it any wonder he was hooked on her? Maybe, if he could convince her to stay in Hawaii for a few more days, they could go snorkeling over there together.

She frowned. "I should be creeped out that you were watching me so closely."

"Correction. You should be flattered, because unlike our photographer, I'm not a stalker. This guy was watching you from up on the overlook bar."

"Which would've been closed at that hour," she said, thinking it through.

"Yes. So it should be easier for your team to find some kind of evidence on the security system."

She took her phone, her fingers flying as she sent the information on to her team. The reply came back in less than a minute. "Claudia says thanks."

She turned her phone so he could see. "All caps," she added with a wry smile. "What now?" She gazed up at the green canopy overhead. "Do we hide here or back at the resort?"

It was obvious she wasn't eager to hunker down and hide until this was over. And, considering the persistent pursuit, he didn't think Welker would stop just because they got away again. They seemed determined to take Cassie out.

Pleasant as it was out here alone with her, safe from any threat, staying was a selfish option.

Going back to the resort was also self-serving. He knew himself too well. With privacy and a bed close by, he'd be doing his best to turn hot kisses into scorching sex.

"There's a third option." He smiled at her wary expression. "Wait a minute." He studied her face, the soft flutter of her pulse at the base of her neck. "Are you thinking about having wild sex with me out here?"

"No."

He leaned in close, until his lips feathered over her ear. "Liar."

"I kissed you, for all the good it did."

Not the response he'd anticipated. The woman was delightfully unpredictable. "Cassie." He stroked her cheek and tipped up her chin, waiting for her to meet his gaze. "If I could, I'd spend days kissing you. And much, much more, if you were so inclined. But until we know *why* Welker is hunting you, we can't forget the risks."

Her phone chimed from her pocket and he wondered which of them was more relieved.

"It's Claudia."

That's all he got as his cell started ringing. He glanced at the caller ID. "Waylen?"

"Where the hell are you?"

"Don't you know?" If the call had come through, surely Waylen had a location on him. More important to Lane at the moment was the stress in his friend's voice. "What's wrong?"

"Hawk has GPS on the Wrangler. He called me asking what the hell you're up to."

Crap, he hadn't sent updates to Hawk or Swann. "I'll take care of it."

"Are you good?"

"For the moment." He put a few paces between himself and Cassie. "She doesn't know why she's been targeted."

"It's gotta be Knowles or the connection to the Pentagon," Waylen suggested.

"She's off that case, the family's out of reach. If Knowles is the issue, they should've shifted their attacks to the new team."

"Then she's holding back," Waylen pointed out. "I'll keep looking."

"No. Don't do that." Lane was her bodyguard, it was his job to earn her trust and get her to open up.

Factoring in his personal interest, he wanted Cassie to open up on her own. "Keep looking into Welker." That was the place Lane couldn't access with his skills. "Please."

"Sure thing." Waylen didn't sound particularly enthused.

"Is there trouble?"

"On this island?" Waylen snorted. "Plenty to go around. You watch over your new friend. And call Hawk."

The call ended, leaving Lane to wonder what the hell his buddies were dealing with, aside from the active volcano crisis. But Waylen was right. Lane's hands were full with the team hunting the woman he was falling in love with.

As the thought flitted through his mind, he tried to dismiss it. To ignore it. Being in love was crazy and about as far from safe as a man could get. But it was true. His feelings for Cassie weren't like anything he'd ever experienced. Strange how he knew that, how he recognized what it was. More astounding was that he could fall so hard after a little danger and a few hotter-than-sin kisses.

Cassie had perched herself on the tailgate of the Wrangler, her gaze on the wilderness while she tapped her phone against her knee. He walked over, somehow keeping his hands to himself. "Any news?"

She wrinkled her nose. "Claudia found my computer in a pawn shop. I offered to pick it up, but she's already arranged to have it shipped back to the Chicago office."

She sounded devastated over being benched yet again. "She doesn't want you involved in case it's another trap," he pointed out.

"Probably." She rubbed her hands on her pants, leaving behind streaks of dirt and dried blood.

"Was the laptop damaged?"

She shook her head. "According to the pictures she received, it's in perfect condition. No one has even tried to log in."

"Another distraction, like Josie's kidnapping." Another attempt to draw Cassie to a place where they could get to her. Not cool. There had to be a way to put a stop to this.

"Apparently so."

There was more, he could see it in her eyes and the set of her mouth. "What else?"

"She moved us to a different part of the resort."

"Us?"

"Yes." Her cheeks puffed up as she blew out a dramatic sigh. "She pulled strings to upgrade your room to one of the condos deeper in the resort. The resort staff packed up your things and mine and just got it done." She paused. "You didn't have anything, *um*, sensitive in the room, did you?"

"No," he replied, wondering what ideas made that blush color her cheeks. "I came to Hawaii for a vacation and a party." He was on a permanent vacation and the weapons he carried were in a locked compartment of his suitcase. No one who knew him would accuse him of being sensitive, much less having any sensitive items or info.

"And you got stuck with me."

"Again, not at all how I would describe the situation." He shifted closer, catching her hand in his. Turning it over he frowned. "Hold that thought."

He went to grab his bottle of water and the first aid kit. "Can't do anything for the pants, but we can take care of these scrapes." He set the first aid kit on the bumper as he rinsed her hands and gently scrubbed the debris off her palms. Rolling up her pant legs, he cleaned the scrapes on her knees next.

"I could do this myself."

"Sure you could." He smiled. "But then I wouldn't have an excuse to touch you."

She stilled his hands. "You don't need an excuse, Lane."

He was caught in those amazing eyes, uncertain how much to push or retreat. His pulse kicked, yearning to get lost in her. "I might." He didn't want to take advantage of the situation or the woman. "What changed?"

"Nothing." She kissed him, her lips light and teasing. "Maybe everything. Just kiss me right here," she tapped her lips, "and make it better."

Never let it be said that he couldn't take orders. He moved between her knees, carefully drawing her legs tighter to his hips. This interlude was nothing short of a miracle. He made the most of it as his mouth claimed hers. Slow and tender, the heat building with every heartbeat. He toyed with her hair, traced the delicate column of her neck down and away over the curve of her shoulder. Her skin was warm and soft, a contrast to the cool, tough security expert she showed the world.

Her hands roamed over him and her soft sigh was the best reward.

If she wanted a distraction, he could provide that. Be that. He wanted more and nearly admitted it. Not the time to dump his unexpected feelings on her. Now while she was in limbo with her career and her life.

He couldn't recall a time when he'd been more than the one-night-stand guy. The sexy, short-term fling that burned bright and flamed out fast. Cassie deserved more, and for the first time Lane thought he might deserve more too.

It shouldn't bother him if her affection was based on an adrenaline surge. He would damn sure be whatever she needed.

Friend, protector, lover.

For Cassie, he was all-in.

11

*C*assie was giving serious thought to that wild sex in the rainforest suggestion when a voice pulled her back, just a little. Reminding her how they'd gotten here.

They were in trouble. Well, she was and Lane, by default, was caught up as well. If she cared about him at all, she should find somewhere else to be. Find another way to flip Welker's plans so she survived and they went to jail for crimes committed.

Then Lane's hands, brushing up along her ribcage, almost to her breasts, drew her focus back where she wanted to be.

With him.

To hell with the rest of the world and all its problems. *This* was paradise—one she hadn't known existed. And it was all because of Lane. He made her feel beautiful and desired. She smoothed her hands up and down his arms, across his chest, eager for that first touch of skin. Her mind was full of visions of how great they'd be together. Had been since that first kiss. Every time he touched her, she wanted more. The scariest thought was wondering if she would ever get enough of Lane.

This was new territory for her, and she didn't mean the island. She felt as if she was in the midst of an emotional earthquake. Out of her depth, uncertain of the next step.

She always knew the next step.

She'd invested the time to be fit, proficient with a number of weapons, and an expert in protection tactics and various skills, including hand to hand combat and defensive driving. She had a knack for situational awareness and strategy and, until this operation had gone sideways, she'd been satisfied with her life. Proud of who she'd become.

And now this. Him.

Lane made her *feel*. *Everything*. From the soft breeze moving over her skin and through her hair to the heat radiating from his body. She would've sworn she could feel the green leaves and blue sky overhead.

It sounded so sappy, even in her own mind, yet she was done shying away from this previously ignored layer of herself. The feminine and fun elements she kept locked down when she was on an assignment. Lane hadn't just sparked an easy or predictable desire. No, he'd triggered an inferno. She'd never been so willing to throw herself headlong into temptation. He'd asked what had changed and though he deserved an answer, she wasn't ready to share more than her body.

That's what he'd first been interested in and that could be enough. Lane wasn't like anyone she'd spent time with before. And all the feelings racing through her system, each of them with their own agendas, left her reeling.

The voice sounded again and she realized it was coming from the radio. This time the words registered, breaking through the sensual haze. "Any available personnel, we could use an assist." The message relayed the name and address of a high school opening up as a shelter.

She pressed a hand to Lane's chest and reluctantly broke away from his kisses. "That's Hawk," she said. "We should go help."

Lane's strong hands glided to her hips, rested there, as he studied her face. "You're serious."

It wasn't a question. He didn't sound annoyed, more curious. He looked oddly satisfied. With himself or her? Did it matter?

She stroked her palms over his strong forearms. It was impossible to be this close and keep her hands to herself. "Why did I ever resist you?"

That cocky grin flashed, then settled into a gentler expression she hadn't seen on his handsome face before. "No idea." He brought her hands to his lips, then lifted her down from the tailgate. "I'm glad you gave in, though." He kissed her softly. "Let's go."

"Just like that?" she asked, moving around to the passenger seat.

He settled behind the wheel and started the engine. While she plugged the address into the navigation app on her phone, he radioed Hawk that they would pitch in. "Did you want to argue about it?"

"Of course not. I guess I expected you to complain that it wasn't a safe option."

"We'll know soon enough if we've made a mistake," he allowed. "We'll take action if needed. This was going to be my suggestion," he continued. "That we find a way to pitch in somehow. But your mind was on wild jungle sex."

She laughed. "Because?"

He shifted in the seat, adjusting his grip on the steering wheel. "It's always served me to be proactive whenever possible. You've got plenty of trouble on your heels and we'll stay alert for sure. But this island is in crisis. Sometimes stepping away from a personal issue and finding a way to give back brings fresh insight or clarity."

That revealing speech wasn't something she'd ever thought to hear from the man who'd flirted with her out on the beach. Moved beyond words, she reached over and rested her hand on his thigh, pleased when he laced his fingers through hers.

They held hands like that, except when he needed to shift gears, all the way to the school.

It was a closeness, a degree of intimacy she hadn't experienced in years. She liked it, liked this connection to Lane. Which seemed strange. She felt simultaneously content and out of her league right now and she thought, watching him weave his hand with hers again, that he might feel the same way.

She tried to recall holding hands with a date or boyfriend and... Couldn't. Her last date had been a while ago, before being assigned to the Knowles family. Wow. That was eye-opening. She'd made sacrifices for her career, but had she given up on a personal life altogether? That was an unpleasant revelation.

She was grateful when they reached the school about an hour later without any issues. Once they were parked, she and Lane climbed out of the Jeep. She headed for the main doors, but he went to the tailgate.

"Problem?"

"I intend to be armed with more than my phone this time." He quickly tucked a handgun into a holster at the small of his back, hiding it behind his shirt. Smiling, he gestured to the door. "Let's dive in."

She hesitated, her hand sliding to her pocket for

her phone. "Do you think Welker is tracking our cell phones?"

"I wouldn't put it past them. They didn't follow us or find us earlier." He tipped his head to the lock-box. "You want a gun?"

"Yes." But she stopped him when he tried to move in that direction. "No, thanks."

"Cassie?"

"I'm waffling. Sorry." She straightened her shirt. "No is my final answer." She was scraped up and her pants were torn. That would draw more attention and she didn't want anyone to notice the bulge of gun at her waist or her ankle. There were signs at the door that weapons weren't allowed inside. "Let me tell Claudia what's going on here."

Once she sent the text, they walked inside to help the folks organizing the space. She was directed to the group setting up cots in long rows across the gleaming gymnasium floor. Each cot needed a blanket, bottle of water, and a personal care bag. Cassie and Lane joined what was basically a bucket brigade, moving up and down the rows with supplies, making sure the cots were ready before the people displaced by the volcano arrived.

She wasn't surprised that Lane insisted on working closely with her. He was subtle about it and *that* was enlightening. More layers, each one more interesting than the last. She'd clearly made assumptions about him out on the beach. Assumptions he'd encouraged, so she wasn't entirely to blame.

The difference between then and now was astounding. If anyone asked, she wouldn't be able to explain it, but she was sure this man at her side was the real Lane. The carefree—almost careless—guy was a facade to keep people at arm's length. What did it mean that he dropped that mask so completely with her?

She wanted to ask, though this wasn't the right place. And she wasn't sure she had the courage. She'd gladly charge into the fray to save a client or friend, but her bravery stopped there. Was she wearing a mask too? She resisted the obvious answer. So what if her personal stuff stayed inside, coming out only for specific therapy sessions?

Except she'd opened up to Lane about all those harsh details and memories from losing her parents. Sharing hadn't felt terrible and his story about his mother had felt like a gift.

"What's that face about?" Lane asked as they walked back to the volunteer table for their next assignment.

"Nothing really." She flicked her wrist, wishing she could cast off this curious heaviness around her heart. "My mind's wandering." What a lie. Her mind was on Lane and not much else.

"Do we need to go?" His brow furrowed,

shading those pale blue eyes. "Did you think of something?"

"No and no." She gave his shoulder a squeeze. "Let's focus on what's in front of us. There's more to do."

Although he didn't seem convinced by her answer, he didn't push. She knew the reprieve would be short lived. He was hoping she'd figure out why Welker was after her. Maybe if she actually gave that some thought, she'd come up with something. But it was far more pleasant to focus on Lane.

He handed her a water and an energy bar and they paused long enough to wolf down the snack. She watched him chat with other volunteers, asking questions about life on the Big Island. If she didn't know better, she'd think he was considering a more permanent stay. But he was the fun-loving vacation guy, squeezing every ounce out of his retirement.

From her pocket, her cell phone sounded with the ringtone she'd assigned to Claudia's number. "Hello?" she answered, stepping back from the group.

Lane extricated himself from his conversation, moving with her.

"Are you alone?" Claudia asked. "I mean, I know where you are and what you're doing, kind of. Can you listen?"

"Yes." Her skin chilled. Something was wrong. Something big. "Just tell me."

"Drake died," Claudia blurted. "I'm so sorry, Cassie."

She couldn't believe it. "What? No." Her breath stalled out and her vision turned dark around the edges. "No. He was fine this morning. Improving." Denial washed over her, dragging her down. "No," she repeated.

The sinking sensation was her own doing. Her knees had buckled, her entire body felt numb, and Lane was easing her into a folding chair. The metal was cold enough to chill her legs through the fabric of her pants, a stiff contrast to the warmth of Lane's palm on the back of her neck.

"What is it?" he murmured.

She shook her head, unable to repeat the dreadful news.

"Put Lane on," Claudia directed. "Cassie. Give the phone to Lane."

She pushed the device toward him, her vision too hazy to know if he took it. This wasn't happening. She must've dozed off and fallen into a nightmare. Drake couldn't be dead. It didn't make any sense at all. Any second now she'd wake up and find herself hiding in the rainforest.

Wrong. She was here, failing as a volunteer, as pain crushed her.

Drake was her partner. Her friend. His recent mistakes were a speedbump, nothing he couldn't come back from.

The mistakes that had made her so angry and put Josie in jeopardy. Cassie suddenly wondered if her last words to him had been kind or cruel. She really should know the answer. Her mind spun and her heart was heavy in her chest. Sluggish.

Then, somehow, she was moving. An arm, warm and firm around her waist, kept her upright.

She blinked when they stepped into the bright afternoon sunlight. "Lane?"

"Right here."

"I want to sit down." She wanted—*needed*—to stop. To make all this nonsense upending her life stop. At least until she could catch her breath.

"Just a second. Almost to the car. You've got this."

"No. I don't." She didn't have anything. No assignment, no partner, no friend. Suddenly, she was swept up off the ground, cradled in Lane's arms. She cuddled in close, grateful for this beautiful, capable man.

"We shouldn't be friends," she mumbled.

"All right." He settled her into the passenger seat and buckled the seatbelt. He wiped a tear from her cheek. "You'll be fine," he assured her, tucking a blanket around her legs. His confidence was soothing, though she wasn't entirely convinced. Her hands started trembling and she couldn't make them stop. Not when Lane held them tightly. Not when he released her and started the car.

She pressed her palms together, under the blanket. It was one of the blankets meant for those coming to the shelter. Guilt swamped her. Everywhere she went, she caused trouble.

The colors were a blur as Lane drove, she couldn't seem to focus on any one thing. Drake was dead. He was dead and she'd never have a chance to reconcile. She'd failed her partner. That was the critical mistake. She had to do better. For Drake's memory, for herself, and for Lane if he was staying on as her bodyguard.

"I should've been there. For Drake. To protect him."

"Agree to disagree," Lane said, his voice low. "Guy made his own choices. Sticking around for the fallout wasn't an option," he reminded her. At the next stop light, he took the cap off a bottle of water and held it out to her. "Take a sip."

The cool liquid helped a little. "Got anything stronger?"

His mouth twitched. "Not in the car." The light changed and his gaze returned to the road. "We'll be at the new place soon. Claudia told me the condo is stocked."

"Good."

He glanced at her. "You're perking up."

"Yeah." The initial shock was fading. After a minute, she recognized the street they were on. "Did

I sleep?" They were closer to the resort than she expected.

"I wish," he said. "You've been staring mostly."

That sounded creepy. "Sorry."

He reached over and gripped her hand. "Don't you dare apologize. Grief sucks, we both know that."

"True." And her complete meltdown was hard evidence. She plucked at the blanket covering her legs. "Thanks for the assist."

"Anytime, anywhere, I'm yours."

He said it as if it was a vow. She frowned. "Is that a line?"

"Not one I've ever used before," he said. "Unless you count my SEAL ops."

That sounded remarkably like a confession. One that sent a curious sparkle through her system. She believed him. His actions certainly backed up the words. Time and again, he'd been there for her. If she wasn't careful, she'd be in love with him before this was over. Was that crazy? It had to be.

And yet, it didn't feel wrong. Didn't even make it less true.

He turned off the main road, onto a tree lined drive that curved gently to the west. When the trees parted, a rainbow arched across the sky. Rainbows were a frequent sight in Hawaii and yet right now it felt like her own private miracle. A sign of hope to thaw out that chill of sorrow.

Eventually.

A few minutes later, they were through the gated entrance and on their way to the condo. "This is more secure than the resort tower?"

"Your team thinks so," Lane said. "We'll trust them."

She was glad he seemed to know exactly where to go. As she took in the area, she was grateful for Claudia's initiative. With the wide streets and open areas between each group of condos, they would certainly be able to see a threat coming.

"We're the only reservation in these four units for the next few days," Lane said, parking in front of a two-story building. "We'll have plenty of privacy and know immediately if someone doesn't belong," he explained.

"Do you think Welker killed Drake?"

"It's crossed my mind," Lane admitted as he hopped out of the Wrangler. "Claudia wants you to call once we're inside." He was standing in front of her, holding out a hand.

She gratefully accepted the support. "Thanks." She managed to keep it at that when everything inside her wanted to apologize. There was no need for that. Lane understood what she was going through.

They walked upstairs to the condo and, using the code Claudia had sent, unlocked the door. Inside, a ceiling fan turned slowly over a sitting area and a wall of windows overlooked a stunning, expansive view. Cassie walked through the rooms, looking around. In the primary bedroom, she found her suitcase unzipped and open on a luggage rack. Lane's luggage was in the closet and his clothing on hangers and in the drawers. Whoever moved them here didn't realize they weren't a couple.

What were they?

Friends who kissed, she decided. Except Lane had said something about not being friends.

Hearing Lane curse, she hurried out of the bedroom. She could move her suitcase to one of the other rooms later. Cassie found him in the kitchen staring into the open refrigerator. "She wasn't kidding about having things stocked," he said. "Come look. There has to be something here you want to eat."

She'd been sure she wasn't hungry until Lane pulled out trays of fruit and cheese. He tipped his head toward the counter. "We have something stronger than water now. Beer and wine too."

Cassie gaped at the bottles of vodka, rum, and tequila. When she had liquor, it was either vodka or rum. "You drink tequila?"

He nodded.

"Claudia always knows."

"Lucky for us."

Lane fixed plates for each of them and Cassie followed him to the balcony. The wind was once

189

again steering the ash cloud away from this side of the island.

"I keep wondering about the last thing I said to him," she admitted. "I don't think it was nice."

"It wasn't anything rude," Lane said. "You said "we're leaving" and walked out."

"And he told us to watch our backs."

Lane nodded. "Turns out it was good advice."

She sighed, not excited about agreeing with him. "But we're no closer to knowing why Welker is after me." She pushed her plate away.

"We'll figure it out." He nudged her plate back in front of her. "Keep eating."

She frowned at the plate, then at him, but it only bounced off his charming smile. Picking up a slice of papaya, she decided cooperating was the better choice. She'd been mean to Drake and lost any chance to make it right. Best not repeat the mistake with Lane.

12

*L*ane congratulated himself for getting some food into Cassie, even if the meal was light. She'd gone into shock so fast over the news about Drake. It had scared the crap out of him to watch such a capable woman crumble.

If there had been any doubts about the stress of the situation, he had his answer.

She'd taken it all on her shoulders and was stuffing it deep down. She needed to let it go. From the unanswered questions to the grief, she needed a break. So when she stretched out on the couch and fell asleep, he wanted to celebrate.

Instead, he opened his laptop and got to work. He took his time drafting the updates for her boss and Hawk. After a careful review of the most recent events, he hit send.

He reached out to Claudia for any additional details on either Drake, the feds, or Welker Specialists. He reached out to Waylen too. When neither of them replied instantly, he combed through the news reports on the incident at the hospital.

It was too early for an obituary on Drake, but on a whim, he googled the man's name to see if anything helpful showed up. Another bust. However his life connected with Greenlee, it wasn't online where Lane could find it.

Which left him with what?

He sat back and cracked his knuckles, thinking. Before he could second guess it, he did a search for Welker Specialists. His cyber skills weren't on par with Waylen or Claudia, but maybe he could find something that would click for Cassie when she woke up.

Just searching the website made him feel gross with the bogus mission statement and the testimonials of satisfied clients. Objectively, he got it. No one wanting to stay in business emphasized their failings or complaints.

How many corporate clients had fallen for this slick presentation?

Lucky for him, many of the reviews included the company names. Lane poked around the companies with offices in D.C., making a list. Then he searched those companies for any ties to the Pentagon.

Nothing intersected with what he knew about Cassie.

Feeling desperate, he looked for companies with a connection to Iowa, Virginia, and Illinois, places he knew Cassie had spent significant time as a kid, training, or on assignment. Unfortunately, no miracles or grand revelations occurred.

Until he clicked through the photo gallery. Faced with too many images of Welker Specialists looking tough and impervious, Lane was too busy rolling his eyes to see it at first. Then he went back through and spotted a face that looked familiar.

The man in the photo wasn't bald and his biceps weren't as overdeveloped, but Lane recognized the shooter at the hospital today. The caption labeled him as Troy Welker, son of the company founder and brother of the current company president. According to the bio, after a decorated career —Lane snorted—Troy no longer led field ops.

Since when did glorified pseudo-bodyguards receive medals for service? And what the hell was the man doing all the way out here?

He sent a screen capture to both Claudia and Waylen, along with a short message confirming Troy's presence in Hawaii.

A few minutes later, his phone rang, and the Caller ID showed Claudia's name. "Hello?" he answered in a whisper.

"Bad time?"

Lane slipped out to the balcony and slid the glass door closed. "No," he replied, still keeping his voice low. "Cassie's sleeping on the couch. Didn't want to wake her."

Claudia didn't reply immediately. "Grief?"

"Yes." He felt bad for giving up secrets Cassie might want to keep. "She's coming around, though. Just worn out."

"This sucks," Claudia grumbled, darkly.

"Do you know who killed him?" Lane's money was on Welker.

"The official word is natural causes."

He paused, sensing a minefield ahead. In his experience, when people tossed the word "official" into a conversation, it was a sure sign of trouble.

"Thanks for being there for her."

The appreciation was thoughtful, but it made his shoulders twitch. At this point, he'd be here and do anything for Cassie. A pretty big mindset shift and a serious declaration for a man who'd been avoiding any sort of constraint for the last six months.

"You find anything on Troy?" Lane asked, attempting to get back to a safer topic. "I'm no research genius, but I can't find any connection between that bastard and Cassie. If she knows anything, she's not sharing it with me." He didn't believe she was willfully hiding anything. She'd been remarkably honest with him from the start. He scrubbed at his jaw and repeated the question he'd been asking all along. "Who gains if Cassie's eliminated?"

Claudia sighed. "Looking at the big picture since her assignment to Judith Knowles, it's clear things have deliberately escalated."

Escalated. Lane swore. "There's a pretty word for attempted murder. To what end?" When Claudia didn't reply, Lane spit out a theory. "I think Greenlee was supposed to kill both her and Drake and be the big hero to bring Josie home. Welker Specialists to the rescue. But he failed. Worse, his ties to Welker put the company in jeopardy."

"Wouldn't be the first time."

"Still, it's a high-profile client and situation. Pentagon employee, child endangerment. Have they ever gone that far on American soil?"

"Not that I've found."

Exactly. "Then whoever dreamed up this plan has to nip the loose ends. Based on what I saw on the website, I'd bet this was Troy's idea and he's scrambling to get it contained before big brother finds out."

He heard what sounded like a pen tapping a desktop. He gave himself points for giving the research expert a viable scenario and making her think. "He's on this island," Lane said. "Leaving isn't easy with the active volcano. Find him and let me handle it."

"How? You're not a SEAL any longer, Lane."

"You're wrong, Claudia." Retirement hadn't dulled his specific skillset. He turned as Cassie stepped out onto the balcony. "Get me a location."

Ending the call, he set his phone aside and smiled. "How was your nap?" She looked soft and sleepy and he wanted to hold her.

She shrugged. "You look as if you're ready to go to war."

"Only for you." He opened his arms. "Need a hug?"

"I won't turn it down."

He let her come to him, willing himself to dial down the vengeful cravings pulsing through his system. Her fingertips skimmed over his bristly jaw and something flickered in her eyes. Not fear, almost a resignation. "You left your laptop open," she said, her arms moving to circle his waist.

He glanced over her head, his hand moving up and down her spine. "Had to send an update on our situation."

"Anything I need to know?"

"Right now?"

Her cheek brushed his chest as she nodded.

He could hardly confess what was really on his mind. All he could think about was how much he wanted her. He loved kissing her, longed for the right to strip away her clothing and discover all of her and everything that made her sigh and moan.

His mind was locked up with a sex-math equation. There were three different bedrooms in this condo, along with two roomy showers, the couches, even the chaise just a few steps away. Not to mention the kitchen counters and floor.

He wanted her on any and all of those surfaces. If she was willing.

Her palms rested quietly on his back, even as his hands cruised over her. She'd just lost her partner, a man she'd counted as a friend. She'd come to him for comfort.

Which made him a top-tier jerk for thinking about sex. Unfortunately, as his hand drifted over her hip once more, he didn't want to think about anything else.

"Lane?"

He'd gone quiet. Well, that wasn't exactly true. His body seemed to hum all around her. He just wasn't talking. His heartbeat was strong and steady under her ear, his hands were drifting up and down her spine, into her hair, and over her curves. Hip to breast and back down again. And the arousal nudging her belly was telling her a great deal.

It was a slow, steady seduction and her body responded to each gentle touch. It was as if he ignited something deep within. A glow that lifted slow and sure until it surfaced, eager for more.

"I'm right here."

She was well aware. She could've asked him for details on whatever he and Claudia had been discussing. Could've pressed for what he hoped to learn from the Welker Specialists website. Instead, a different need filled her, chased by a faint fear that if she didn't make a move, she'd miss out on something remarkable.

She lifted her face from the firm wall of his chest. The tension in his jaw had eased. That was a good sign that his mind wasn't preoccupied with Welker or anything outside of this moment. "Will you kiss me?"

She didn't need to ask twice. He lifted her into his body and claimed her mouth. Slowly, tenderly, it turned into the best kiss of her life. A delightful conclusion, considering their previous kisses.

His scent washed over her, into her. She sighed, her hands slipping under the hem of his shirt to the heated skin she'd been longing to explore.

He twitched, shifting her hands down and away to his hips.

In the haze of desire, it took her a second. "You're ticklish," she accused.

His mouth blazed a path down her throat. "Is that a deal-breaker?"

She was more than half afraid nothing about

Lane would be a deal-breaker for her. "Not at all," she managed as his tongue teased the shell of her ear. Shivering, she distantly wondered why that suddenly felt so good. "How should I touch you?"

"However you want." The words rumbled against her skin. "I'll be fine."

She wanted him to be way better than fine. Tugging at his shirt, she got it off, and just started, overcome by the view of his muscled torso. Of course, she'd seen him on the beach, knew he was fit and tan.

Hot.

On the beach, he hadn't been close. Hadn't been hers. A bold claim she didn't dare speak. But she wanted him to feel it. Feel what he meant to her already. Drawing his head down for more kisses, she stroked his shoulders, the hard planes of his back and lower still. The man had a great butt.

She giggled at herself and he pulled back. "Problem?"

"No." It dawned on her that they were outside and she suddenly felt too exposed. "Let's go in."

"And?"

She blinked at his heated gaze. "And have wild sex in the bedroom."

To her delight, he boosted her up into his arms and hustled them inside, pausing only long enough to lock the door. They laughed, between lengthy kisses, all the way to the bedroom.

She'd never felt so fizzy or happy when sex was on offer. But that was all the thought she could give to the past. The present had her full attention.

Lane was front and center and stripping away her clothing. His gaze made her pulse skip and desire consumed her. Weak-kneed, she sat on the edge of the bed in only her bra and panties, reaching for him. Needing him.

This craving was real and raw and shocking. "Lane."

He stretched out on the bed with her, his fingers light in her hair. "I'm here for you, Cass."

She knew he understood. Heard the same tremors in his voice that were rolling through her body. Maybe he even felt as awed by this as she did.

"Just kiss me," he said, echoing her request when they'd been hiding.

Those three words were all she needed. Emboldened, she claimed his mouth, then let herself discover all of him, mindful of any ticklish places amid the hard, impervious planes and sharp angles.

He brought her over him, teasing and sucking her nipples through the sheer lace of her bra until the tips were impossibly tight. She was wet and ready and wouldn't last another five minutes at this rate.

She arched into him, desperately excited for the pleasure he lavished on her, even as she longed to touch him everywhere. Fumbling with the button and zipper of his pants, he took over and while he shed the last of his clothing she wriggled out of her panties.

He stared so intently she started to wonder what was wrong.

"Your tan lines."

She reached to cover them.

"Don't." His voice was rough and her blood raced with anticipation. "I want your secrets, Cass." He traced the pale lines where her bikini had blocked the sun, tormenting her with his fingers and mouth, even his beard. "These places are just for us."

Settling himself between her legs, he licked her slick folds. Her hips bucked and he caught her hips, holding her steady.

Or as steady as she could be as he lapped and teased with an exquisite touch, taking her to the edge over and over, until she was begging for release. For him. "Lane, please," she gasped. Her body ached for him and at last he drove her to a climax that left her limbs quivering.

It was glorious and left her breathless. And still, she needed more. Him.

Again, he seemed to know.

She tried to catch her breath as he rolled a condom over his erection and came over her. If he'd wanted to go slow, it would have to be the next time.

She was out of patience, her body feeling too hollow. The only satisfaction was Lane.

She pushed him back and straddled his hips, sinking down over his shaft in one fast, smooth glide. He growled out her name, his fingertips tight on her hips. He fit perfectly, as if they'd been made for each other. She leaned forward to claim his mouth. Then she had to move, riding him until she hit that peak again. Her heart thundered in her chest, pleasure coursing through her in wild pulses.

She gasped as he took over, rolling her back while still buried deep. She gripped his arms, needing the anchor as he thrust into her. Her gaze locked with his, she matched his pace, her legs tight on his hips, her body clenching him with every stroke. This time when she climaxed, he was with her, her name a ragged shout on his lips.

Nothing had ever sounded so sweet.

She didn't want to let go of the man or the moment.

He kissed her with such tenderness she worried she'd cry. As he got up to deal with the condom, she was grateful for a chance to gather her composure. Her body was satisfied beyond compare and although her emotions were still a bit frayed, she felt perfect, inside and out. As if she'd found something precious and the discovery shaped her into a better version of herself.

She resisted further introspection as Lane joined

her in the bed. In his arms, her body relaxed, she reveled in the bliss and contentment he'd given her.

In the aftermath, feeling equally wrecked and energized, Lane wound a lock of her hair around his finger. Cassie's body was warm and soft against his, but he could tell she was still awake.

"Can I ask a favor?"

She gave a satisfied hum that only revved him up again. As she rolled to her side, the smile on her face was feminine and lovely and utterly tantalizing. She reached up and traced a finger along his jaw. "After that, you can ask me anything."

He caught her fingertip lightly between his teeth before kissing her again. The woman was irresistible. And with that open invitation, a thousand questions rushed through his mind. Later. There would be time to ask her everything. He'd make sure of it.

"Lane? What's the favor?"

"Right." He dragged his gaze away from her mouth and back to her amazing eyes. "Can we leave this particular detail out of the daily update?"

Her eyebrows arched. "Are you asking me to falsify the day's activity report?" She made a tsking sound. "That doesn't sound like the above-board, honorable thing to do."

Be still my heart. She was flirting with him. Cassie, the stoic woman who insisted character and integrity trumped charm, was flirting. His pulse kicked. He wanted her again. Right now. He nudged her over, covering her body with his and running kisses up and down her throat.

"We'll talk about it later."

She arched into him, her fingernails skating over his shoulders. "Much later."

This would be enough. More than enough. After the attacks, the grief, and the unknowns, he was okay with forgetting all of it in favor of the wonder of having her in his arms. In his heart.

13

---

*C*assic woke up to the muted light of early morning filtering through the gauzy curtains covering the big windows in the bedroom. She was tangled with the incomparable heat of Lane, snuggled skin to skin. It was the best morning in recent memory.

She closed her eyes, recalling the wonder of last night, with one pleasure layered over another. Being with Lane had been mind-blowing. Enlightening.

She breathed him in. It probably couldn't last, but she found herself wishing all the same. What would life be like with a real partner? That wasn't a fair question. She didn't want to come home to just any man. Didn't want to be so open and vulnerable with anyone but Lane.

Cultivating a real relationship with him tempted her more than ever before.

Because she loved him.

Love as a concept had always seemed fleeting to her. Resting with it here, with him, feeling the rise and fall of his chest under her palm as he slept, she understood love in a new way. Her heart belonged to him. Wanted him. Love was true. Irrevocable.

Did that make her a sad cliché or a woman who knew her mind?

She really should question such a big leap of her heart within their short acquaintance. And yet, it felt right. Touching her lips softly to his chest, she eased out of the bed, letting him sleep. The first item of clothing she found was his shirt and she slipped it on as she padded to the bathroom.

She was finishing her shower when she heard Lane's voice just outside the door. "One second," he said.

At the knock, she told him to come in as she quickly toweled off.

"Claudia," he murmured, handing her the phone. Then he kissed her cheek as he traded places with her.

"I'm here," Cassie said. "What's wrong?"

"Good news first. I found Troy Welker," she said. "Bad news. Your location is compromised."

"What?"

"I'm sorry." Claudia swore. "If you move fast—like, right now—maybe you can catch *him* off guard rather than be on the defensive."

Cassie could get on board with that idea. Much better than having him storm the condo and put innocent bystanders at risk. "You're sure he's gunning for me?" she asked, heading to the bedroom to dress.

"Absolutely," Claudia said. "Lane too, since he was there when Greenlee attacked you. Troy found the resort employee who moved you to the condo. Beat the kid to a pulp."

Cassie muttered an oath. She thought about the wide open areas around the condos. Those spaces weren't enough to deter Welker.

Putting herself in his shoes, she cringed. Assuming he wanted to minimize the collateral damage and exposure, Troy would subdue the guard at the gatehouse, drive up to the condo, and break in. If he had numbers, he'd use the advantage to kill her and Lane and leave their bodies behind.

Too easy.

Cassie heard the shower shut off. She wouldn't let Troy skate on this. She and Lane had proven an effective team on the zipline trail. With good intel— the only kind Claudia provided—they could turn the tables on Welker.

"How much time do we have?"

"Not much," Claudia said. "So far, I don't have any evidence that will hold up in court," she continued, "but I'm sure Troy sent Greenlee to Hawaii to kill you and Drake. Didn't Lane tell you his theory?"

"We had other things to discuss." And much better things to do. She could feel guilty about it later. This wasn't the time to berate herself for snatching a moment of joy in the middle of this mess.

"Fair enough," Claudia continued. "I know losing Drake was a big blow."

That was putting it mildly. Cassie moved to the windows, searching the view for any signs of trouble.

"Everyone is reeling," Claudia said. "I haven't seen Gamble and Swann this upset in ages."

Cassie let the wave of grief wash over her. Survival first, then closure. She'd make sure Drake's memory was honored. "Clearly Troy is cutting off any and all loose ends."

Claudia agreed. "I've been scrambling to get ahead of this." She paused, only the soft sound of her fingers on the keyboard coming over the line. "We do know Drake was trying to learn whatever Greenlee knew about the issues you were having on the Knowles assignment. Primarily, he was pushing Greenlee to talk about why Welker was causing trouble."

"But you still don't know?"

"No confirmation yet, but I think Troy was trying to prove himself," Claudia explained. "Stay relevant to the company. Lane's theory is that the kidnapping would've painted Welker as heroes and they need the good publicity. I've found some communications that Troy's big brother hasn't been impressed with him hanging around, acting tough, and doing nothing. In my opinion, your access to the Pentagon is no coincidence."

Cassie could see the logic. Troy makes a bold move, takes advantage of a tie between Greenlee and Drake and then has to clean up fast when things go sideways. At the minimum, it made her feel better about her partner. "If you're right, I can stop wracking my brain for when my path crossed Troy Welker's."

"You definitely have better things to do," Claudia said. "I've sent his current location. It's a vacation rental in a residential area south of you. Welker and at least two other men are inside. The guys involved with the smoke bomb at the hospital."

"At least?" Cassie wanted clarification on the numbers.

Lane came out of the bathroom and she turned away so she could focus on the information. He was such a marvelous distraction.

"If he recruited additional local help, they might be holed up in there with him," Claudia said. "Doubtful, but I can't rule it out. I've scoured nearby cameras and that's the best I have."

"Any food deliveries within the last day?" Cassie asked.

"Oh! Great idea. Hold on."

Cassie went to the kitchen and grabbed a couple of Cokes. They didn't have time for coffee if they wanted to maintain an element of surprise, but she needed the caffeine boost. Lane walked out of the bedroom, dressed in a dark blue t-shirt and cargo pants. She put the phone on speaker.

"Here we go," Claudia said. "Food was delivered twice yesterday. One grocery order and a later delivery from a local restaurant. Based on the order, looks like it's Welker and two others."

"Might be better to let them come to us," Lane said.

"Are you kidding?" Cassie stared at him.

"Sounds like you two have more to discuss. Don't take too long," Claudia urged. "Once you have Troy under control, call the FBI office. They'll coordinate with Gamble."

"Was that the FBI at the hospital yesterday?" Cassie bristled. "They should've identified themselves."

"Told you," Lane whispered.

"You know how weird feds can be," Claudia said. "I'll let you know if Troy mobilizes."

"Thanks," Cassie barely got the word out before the call ended. "So. Um. Good morning," she said to Lane.

He glared at the Cokes on the countertop. "We have time for coffee if we let Troy think he has the advantage."

"Are you seriously building a tactical strategy around a cup of coffee?"

Ignoring her, he poured beans into the grinder. She didn't want to admit it, but just the aroma perked her up. When the coffee was brewing he pulled her into his arms, lingering over the kiss. "This is a proper good morning."

"I want it to be." She glanced toward the balcony. "We can't just sit here and wait." She tried to shift away from Lane, but he kept her close. "Lane, he beat up the employee who moved our things here."

"So we'll add that to the growing list of charges." He squeezed her waist. "You and I can't take him down in the middle of a neighborhood."

"This is a neighborhood too." The risks were real no matter where they did this. "Can't we lure him to the volcano and toss him in?"

Lane chuckled. "That's a great visual. And I'd take that option in a heartbeat if there was any hope of success." He rested his forehead on hers. "We are the only guests in this building," he countered. "Welker can't come in here guns blazing without making more trouble for himself."

"So you and I against three mercenaries?"

"Two and a half," Lane corrected. "The newbie he brought along isn't much of a threat." He turned and poured coffee for each of them.

She sipped the hot brew. Coffee was the right

choice. "My boss won't be happy to get the bill for damages if we tear up this condo."

"I thought a couple of lawyers ran the Guardian Agency."

"That's true." She eyed him over her coffee. "You've been doing your homework."

"Grief knocked you out for a while yesterday. Had to fill the time somehow." He gave her a wink. "I think your bosses will make sure Welker Specialists gets the bill for any mess they make here. Plus the invoice to replace your favorite shirt."

"You really want to do this here?" She sipped her coffee, wary as another thought occurred to her. They were both in Welker's crosshairs and she wouldn't let Lane shield her from the fight. She could hold her own and, after what happened to Drake, she intended to face Welker head on. "This isn't some ploy to keep me out of the fight?"

"No. I need you with me."

She suddenly wished he'd spoken those words romantically. Because she definitely needed him. For more than Welker. When this was over, they needed to have a heart to heart. Studying him now, she wasn't sure she trusted his cool composure. "You say that now, but I won't sit back, Lane."

"Aren't you listening?" He stroked her cheek. "I need *you*. I don't want you to sit back. I've seen you in action, remember?"

She wasn't sure if he meant out on the zipline

trail or if that was a reference to last night. She opted to assume the best. "We'll need to work together to finish off Welker." She thought again about the guard at the gatehouse. "How do we protect the guard? I don't want Welker to hurt anyone else."

"Leave it to me." He smiled, but this time the expression was flinty and calculating. His jaw was tight too. Something about the combination settled her better than any amount of planning or conversation.

"All right," she said, refilling her coffee. "And tell me we have more ammunition than what's left in my gun."

"You can count on me, Cassie. And you can count on my friends too."

14

*L*ane realized his mistake as soon as Claudia called. He should've stayed on track and talked to Cassie about this entire mess before giving into passion last night.

What a mood killer that would've been.

Once she'd kissed him, he'd forgotten everything else anyway. He'd felt safe without confirming whether or not it was true. It was a miracle Welker hadn't attacked while they were so vulnerable. Apparently, the bastard had been too busy beating up the resort employee. And now, he was too confident in his advantage. Troy Welker was no strategic genius. He was reactive. An impulsive bully who believed his own press and bravado.

Today would not go his way.

"Kian is at the gatehouse," Lane explained. "He'll let Troy through, or duke it out right there if necessary." Lane really hoped it wouldn't be necessary, because he wanted to deliver Welker to the FBI personally. "Waylen is downstairs with extra firepower."

Cassie's eyes went round for just a moment. "I shouldn't be surprised."

"You shouldn't?" His friends had been. To hear them talk, he was practically the poster child for being unreliable these past months. They weren't entirely wrong.

"No." She grinned at him before ducking into the fridge for something to eat. Pulling out the fruit and cheese, she motioned for him to hand her a couple of plates.

"I need you to elaborate," he said.

"You're fishing for compliments."

"Fishing is Waylen's thing." He watched her plate up a decent breakfast. "Why aren't you surprised?"

"From the start, you've been focused and professional." She tilted her head, her nose wrinkling. "Not from the beach start. From the start of the search for Josie," she clarified. "I admit I was disappointed Hawk sent you, but I was wrong and I recognized it right away."

He chuckled. "Right away, huh? You didn't show it right away."

"I was preoccupied, if you recall."

He recalled. He recalled every single minute

since he'd spotted her on that beach. And although he didn't enjoy the idea of her in any kind of danger, he treasured every second they'd been together.

"Fair enough." His phone buzzed. "That's Waylen." He stuffed a slice of papaya into his mouth, chewing and swallowing in a hurry. "You ready?"

Her phone chimed as well. "Claudia," she said. "Troy is on the move. Three men total. She sent a picture." Cassie came around so they could look at her phone together.

Welker was driving a big SUV, likely loaded with weapons. He was tempted to tip off the local cops, but that probably wouldn't end well. The goal was to avoid injuring more bystanders. Besides, all the first responders on this island were coping with various volcano-induced crises.

It was up to him and Cassie, with the help of Waylen and Kian, to finish this.

"At this early hour, they'll be here in less than twenty minutes."

Cassie nodded, her expression somber. "And once we hand them over to the FBI, we can head for the lagoon and relax."

He suspected they would earn that relaxation. "I like the way you think." He brushed his lips over hers. "It's a date."

"Our first date without any weapons?"

"Yeah. I think that's a good goal."

Shoving aside the happier thoughts of first dates and the implication of second and third dates to follow, he opened the door for Waylen.

"Coffee?" Cassie offered.

"I'm good, thanks." Waylen glanced at Lane, clearly surprised by Cassie's cheery offer. "I brought some extra intel in addition to the ammunition."

"What do you mean?" Cassie retrieved her guns from her luggage and joined them at the dining table.

"A friend of mine is stationed at the Pentagon. I called in a favor based on Lane's theory."

"The theory that Troy Welker is trying to convince his brother not to cut him off?" she asked.

"That's the one," Waylen said. He unzipped a backpack, revealing boxes of ammunition for each of their weapons.

She frowned, peering into the backpack. "Do I want to know?"

"No biggie." Lane handed her a pre-loaded clip for her handgun.

"Hawk keeps a good stock," Waylen confirmed.

Lane could practically see her internal debate. She was second-guessing what they were about to do. "It won't be a shootout." He ignored the skepticism that flitted over Waylen's face, instead focusing on Cassie. "I won't let it come to that."

She shook her head. "It's not entirely your choice. We've seen what Welker's capable of."

"Which is how I know we can stop him," Lane said. "He's not expecting us to have any backup. He believes he has the element of surprise."

"Lane's right," Waylen said. "Guy is cocky as hell. My Pentagon contact knows about a client on the Welker roster who was dissatisfied with the service provided for personal security. Extremely so."

"What happened?" Cassie asked as she finished loading her guns and tucking a spare clip into her pockets.

"Turns out the Welker bodyguard disappeared from his post. He claims he got lost." Waylen rolled his eyes. "In the meantime, the client got caught up in the very altercation they'd hired Welker to prevent. Client was in the middle of a nasty divorce."

"When?" Cassie planted her hands on her hips. "Any idea where the bodyguard went?"

"Oddly enough, my friend has footage of Welker's guy near Mrs. Knowles's offices."

Lane watched the color drain from Cassie's face. "Sit down," he murmured.

She held out a hand, preventing any assistance. "Before or after Drake and I came on board?"

"Before," Waylen replied. "Likely that's one of

the creepy moments that convinced her to hire protection."

A siren sounded, muted, but in the room. Lane waved his hand and pulled out his phone. "That's the alert from Kian at the gatehouse. Troy Welker plus two. We need to get set."

"Right." Waylen pulled out a handful of plastic zip ties. "Don't forget these. I'm sure the feds want these jerks alive."

"I'm sure they do," Cassie muttered. "Drake went home in a body bag. I'll be damned if Welker goes home first class."

Lane saw Waylen's brows arch in admiration of her attitude and smothered his smile. Cassie was feisty and a fighter to the bone. Moreover, she was a survivor. They'd get through this. And it wouldn't come down to a hail of bullets. As much as he wanted to protect her, there was a comfort knowing she could protect herself.

"Kian will move to disable their SUV and cover the front," Waylen said. "I'm out back."

"Make sure they get up here," Cassie called after him. "I want Welker to know exactly who is taking him down."

Lane managed to smother his reaction until Waylen closed the front door. "Don't tell me you'll offer him coffee," he said when they were alone. "I'm not up for some touchy-feely scene. I want a piece of him."

"That makes two of us," she confirmed. "He thinks he has us cornered. Let him believe it."

He followed her back to the bathroom, where she turned on the shower. "Blind canyon ploy. He can't afford a loud scene. He'll leap on the chance to take us in the shower. Once we get them in here, we've got control."

He had to agree with the tactic. And it was too late to change anything. She headed for the closet and he ducked behind the bedroom door.

Lane felt the seconds ticking by. Slowly, each one separated from the next. The familiar sensation often happened during his team missions. His body knew what to do and how to do it.

Objectivity wasn't so easy to maintain this time, even with his pals backing them up. He was edgy because of Cassie. But she needed him sharp. Focused. And as steady as a SEAL should be.

He heard the pop of the lock on the front door breaking. So far, Welker was doing exactly what they'd expected.

The voices were too low to fully understand as they cleared the main, open-concept areas of the condo. Lane could fill in the blanks, having cleared many a building during his career. He waited, wondering what Cassie could hear from the closet.

What he wouldn't give for an earpiece right now. There was nothing so lonely as anticipating the fight without someone chattering in his ear. He wondered if his friends would say the same. It wasn't something they discussed.

Maybe he'd bring it up over drinks some time. Right now, it was showtime.

The leader—had to be Welker—paused at the threshold. He raised his gun, but didn't enter the room. "Shower," he said to the man behind him. "Easier than fish in a barrel."

He lowered his gun, striding forward.

Lane held his position, prayed Cassie would do the same. Once Welker was in the bathroom, she could lock him inside while Lane handled the other two men.

Welker made it to the bathroom and Cassie leapt into action. He'd expected her to pull the door closed, but she followed him inside and slammed the door behind her.

Lane's heart lurched. That wasn't the plan. Except they hadn't planned much of anything. Not in enough detail. No time to dwell on the shouts and sounds as she and Welker fought. He had to subdue the man who'd kept watch at the door. The man stepped forward and Lane slammed the door, knocking the gun out of his hands. To his shock, the man dropped to his knees. "Don't shoot! I'm sorry! Sorry! Don't shoot!"

Had to be a trap. This wasn't the newbie. Lane approached cautiously while the guy kept up the pathetic litany. "Face down," Lane barked.

The guy flopped down, face in the carpet, then suddenly flipped over and sprang to his feet. Lane's stress faded as the guy lunged. *This* was exactly what he needed. He tossed his gun to the bed and let himself get tackled, rolling until he was on top again. With a knee in the guy's diaphragm, he pummeled the guy's face, dodging a few wild blows in the process.

A gun blasted, shattering the sliding glass door behind him. Hell, he'd forgotten about the third man. The first shot was followed by two more bursts. He smelled blood, thankfully not his, as bullets chattered into the walls across the room.

The skirmish in the bathroom suddenly went quiet.

Cassie!

Lane was done screwing around. Using his opponent as a shield, he swiveled around. There was the newbie, on the balcony, his gun shaking. Not good. *Not* good.

"Spotter!" Lane called out. "Welcome to the party."

Lane shoved the man he'd been fighting through the splintered glass door. The momentum took down both men. Lane leapt for the bed. Waylen or Kian would be here any second. They would've mobilized at the first sound of gunfire.

Grabbing his gun, he crashed through the bathroom door, fearing the worst.

Cassie was on the floor, facing away from him. The back of her shirt was soaked with blood.

His heart stopped. Too much blood. She couldn't die. Not here, not over something as stupid as Welker's plans. "How bad?"

She glanced over her shoulder. "Bad."

He hauled her up and away and she blinked rapidly. "No, not me." She gripped his arms. "Not me." She shook him off. "Welker."

The jerk was coughing up blood as Cassie dropped back to his side, applying pressure to what must be the worst injury. Lane called for an ambulance while he analyzed the chaos in the bathroom. Cassie and Welker had gone at it. The mirror was busted up. The glass door of the shower was leaning, off its track, but otherwise intact.

Welker's bald head was bleeding from several cuts. Lane wanted to give Cassie a high five for that alone. His knuckles were raw and one hand was swelling. Cassie must've stomped on it. One eye was already turning purple and the man's nose was crooked. Lane could see Welker had taken a bullet in one arm and another had caught him in the side, under the bulletproof vest he wore.

"Friendly fire. Too bad for me," he said, kneeling. He grabbed Welker's head to look him in the eyes. "You're a damn coward."

"FBI," Cassie said, her breath short. "Call them."

"You are hurt," Lane accused. "What did he do?"

"Not what he came to do," she said. "If he lives, we can visit him in prison and gloat about it then."

She made a good point. He left her to Welker, the man was no threat now, and went in search of Waylen and Kian. As he'd expected, his friends had the other two attackers cuffed and secured to the balcony railing while they awaited the FBI's arrival.

"Well done," he said to his friends.

"Cassie's good?" Kian asked.

"The best," Lane assured him. "Welker didn't stand a chance."

It was over. To his relief and delight, the FBI was on the scene quickly and they didn't waste a lot of time on statements. Lane chalked up that convenience to Claudia and whatever strings the Guardian Agency and Hawk had pulled behind the scenes.

Once the paramedics treated Cassie's minor wounds, they were free to go.

"Where to?" he asked her.

"The resort." She tapped her phone. "Claudia sent me a reservation number. The Guardian Agency is footing the bill for another week, pure vacation time." She tilted her face up to his. "I could use some advice from a vacay expert."

He drew her into his arms. "I know just the guy." His lips feathered over her cheek, her mouth.

"Fair warning, Hawk or the guys might need me to lend a hand as the island recovers."

"Of course. And I'm willing to help where I can."

"We'll see." He wasn't sure he could deal with her charging headlong into another fight. She could hold her own, but she held his heart too. "You were incredible in there."

"You didn't even see anything," she countered.

He swayed a bit, loving the feel of her in his arms. Loving her. "I saw enough." He'd seen her try to save the man who wanted her dead. She was remarkable.

"I know you have a room," she said, her fingers tracing the pattern on his shirt. "But if you want, you could share mine."

"Looking for twenty-four-seven vacation expertise?"

She pressed up closer and he would've sworn he heard her purr. "With you, absolutely."

The sweet, sexy smile that curled her mouth before she kissed him gave him hope that their upcoming first date would be the start of something fantastic and lasting.

EPILOGUE

Five days later...

Cassie did a last-minute check with the camera angle before her conference call with her bosses at the Guardian Agency. Lane had made himself scarce so she could speak candidly. Gamble and Swann knew injuries happened in the line of duty, but she didn't want them to blame her current abrasions for her decision to walk away.

Nothing about the situation with Welker factored into her decision to resign. She was proud of her work. And she'd miss it.

But she had something new and special with Lane and she wanted to give their relationship a real chance. She couldn't do that if she was on the mainland, busy with another assignment while he was here in Hawaii helping his friends.

Within minutes, however, it was clear Gamble and Swann had other plans for this call. They were clearly pleased with the outcome of the Welker case as they heaped praises on her. She should've known they would be on her side, but it made resigning that much tougher.

"You seem to like Hawaii," Gamble observed.

"Yes, sir." At the moment, Lane was the primary perk, but she couldn't say that.

"We've been diversifying our services," Swann said. "After your exemplary effort with the Knowles family, we reached out to the resort. Based on success at other hotels, we are currently negotiating a similar protection office with the resort. We'd like you to take the lead on that office."

She wasn't sure she'd heard him. This was a serious shift in job responsibility. "You're serious."

"Are we misinterpreting the situation?" Gamble asked. "Are you wanting to pursue something different? You've earned a break and the chance to name your terms."

Absolutely not. One thing the Guardian Agency had taught her was that she wasn't built for breaks. The idea of sitting around idly in Hawaii or anywhere else didn't appeal to her. But leaving Lane, for the sake of a job, felt wrong too.

"In a perfect world? Yes, I want a challenging

career. But you don't have to create a position just for me."

She was so glad she'd sent Lane out of the room. If he were here he'd be urging her to just accept the obvious gift without argument. He wasn't exactly wrong. It just felt so strange that so many things were going right after the chaotic Welker situation.

Gamble smiled warmly. "When we get the right people in the right place, we like to keep them there."

"You single-handedly protected not only the client but our business interests," Swann said. "To say we appreciate that is an understatement. It's hard to describe just how much damage control would ensue if Welker had succeeded. We believe in rewarding loyalty."

"Hardly single-handedly," she reminded them. "Without Lane and his teammates and the Brotherhood Protectors resources, things might've gone Welker's way."

She and Drake might both be dead now without all of that support.

"You're making my point," Gamble said. "You know how to rally the right people to your cause. As the lead there at the resort, you'll have final say about the team you build."

"You can take some time——"

"I accept," she said, thinking of Lane. She didn't know if he would stay in Hawaii. They were too busy "dating" to discuss anything long term. But she had the sense that despite all the action, maybe because of it, Lane and his closest friends were thinking about staying. Either way, she trusted her intuition that this was the right move. "Thank you both."

Gamble assured her that her new employment package would be arriving within a day or two and to take her time and ask plenty of questions. Above all, it seemed their first priority was making sure she was happy.

Ending the video call, Cassie sat back in her chair marveling at how much her life had changed in such a short time.

She'd lost a partner, a good man who would be missed.

She'd overcome significant threats to herself, her company, and her career. Thanks to Lane and his friends, she had survived.

More than that.

She'd fallen in love with Lane. Loving him didn't feel scary or wrong. Just the opposite, every day with him felt perfect. Thrilled about the promotion and the possibilities on her horizon, she popped up out of the chair. She had to find him. Had to tell him exactly how she felt.

She couldn't do anything less. How wild was it that she couldn't wait to put her heart in his hands?

Something deep and important inside her understood that Lane was the right guy to trust with her deepest desires and vulnerabilities. With Lane, all of her old fears and issues seemed to fade away. Maybe not completely, but enough that she could see him for who and what he was.

More than her hero, he was her forever.

Body and soul, she knew staying with Lane was the best choice for her. The only choice. Building a life with him, here or anywhere else, would be exciting, occasionally outrageous, and definitely an adventure. And she couldn't wait to get started.

In the hallway outside their hotel room, Lane paced back and forth.

Were her bosses giving her crap? Did she need backup? They had no right to challenge her decisions or critique how she'd handled herself. She'd been assertive and professional from the first moment to the last.

He walked up to the door, keycard at the ready, and caught himself before he barged in. Sure, he'd defend her to the grave, and call in every favor he was owed to help her.

And she wouldn't accept any of that kind of help. Didn't need it. She wasn't just a grown woman. She was smart and more capable than most men he knew. Outside of his team, of course.

Stepping back from the door, he raked a hand through his hair. He just wanted her to be okay. More than okay. He wanted her to be happy. Truly happy. Because her smile was like sunlight breaking through the clouds. The world needed that smile.

He needed that smile.

He stalked down toward the elevators again and turned on his heel.

And if her happiness required her moving on, if she needed to get back to work? He swore under his breath. Well, that would suck, but he would honor her decision.

He rubbed his knuckles against the sudden ache in his chest. His heart sure as hell didn't want to accept a future without Cassie in it.

Too bad. This was about her.

"Lane?" Harlan was striding toward him. "Man, what's wrong with you?"

"Nothing," Lane said, completely locked in denial. "What are you doing here? I thought you'd be—"

Harlan cut him off. "You haven't looked this serious in... well, ever."

"Thanks," Lane grumbled. Sure, he was notoriously the most unserious guy in any situation. Unless they were running an op in the field or he was tucked into a sniper's nest.

"Are you waiting on Cassie?"

He jerked his chin back toward the room. "She's doing the debrief with her bosses."

"Hope she's less stressed than you," Harlan observed.

"I'm fine," Lane denied.

Harlan tapped the phone in his hand, his gaze always analyzing. "You weren't picking up."

Lane reached down, patting the cell phone in his pocket. "Sorry. I silenced it." Because he just couldn't cope with one more interruption and he didn't want to risk being drawn away before he knew the outcome of Cassie's video conference.

How much time did a couple of lawyers need to either give her a promotion or fire her? Then again, lawyers billed by the hour and plenty of them were addicted to their own voices.

"I get it," Harlan said in the tone that had deescalated situations and saved lives around the world. "We're heading over to the bar. I wanted to make sure you and Cassie knew where to find us."

Lane rolled his tight shoulders. He really was too stressed. "Thanks. We'll be there soon."

They would be there, he vowed. Together. To celebrate whatever decision she'd made.

He soothed the erratic beat of his heart with the reminder that they had time. Even if she chose to move on, Cassie wouldn't be leaving right away. The volcano was still causing havoc and disrupting travel in and around the islands.

He knew he was among the few people who were actually thankful for the eruption. The crisis had brought him into Cassie's world. Teaming up with her had given him the purpose he'd been searching for these past six months.

A purpose that went beyond a case or a mission.

It was more than a little unsettling to find that his inner peace was tied so tightly to a woman he'd just met.

The door opened—finally—and for a second he couldn't breathe. She looked so damn happy. Happier than the first time he'd seen her on the beach.

Crap. They must have offered her a promotion.

"Get in here," she said.

He didn't have to be told twice. He kicked the door shut and all the words he wanted to give her got tangled up in his throat and he just stared.

That happiness on her face clouded over with immediate concern. "Are you okay?"

He waved that off. "Yeah I'm fine. Did they give you hell?"

"No."

"Good. Now I don't have to hunt them down," he said, smiling to soften the threat.

She stroked his jaw, her gaze soft and understanding. "I imagine my bosses could take care of themselves. If not, there's plenty of protection between you and them." She tapped her finger on his chest. "Starting with me. Gamble and Swann are two of the best people I know."

"All right." He held his hands up in surrender. The last thing he wanted to hear was her talking about other men. He didn't care how far away they might be. "They gave you a chance when you needed one. I get that." He tried to stay casual about it all, even with his heart thundering in his ears. "So spill. What's the news?"

She nipped her lower lip. "Well, I'm just going to say it. I'm not expecting any specific response from you." She peered up at him through her eyelashes.

He was pretty sure his heart stopped. "I'm listening."

"They gave me a job here. At this resort. If I want it."

It took him a second. The warning had made him think she was going to tell him something far more personal. "You'd have a permanent assignment here on the Big Island?" He wanted to be very specific about this.

"Yes. I'd be leading a personal security office here at the resort. I get to build my own team."

He heard her list off the details and the benefits and the responsibilities, but her voice seemed to fade as if she wasn't sure about taking the job. "You don't look happy," she finished.

"Do you really want this job?" he queried. "Because you seemed happy as hell a minute ago and now *you* don't look so sure. I want you to be happy, Cass."

She kissed him quickly. "Yes. I want this job. It's more than I could've hoped for. Working in paradise, having stability, and backed by one of the best security agencies around." She planted her hands on her hips. "You're still scowling at me? I thought you would help me celebrate."

"Of course I will. The guys invited us to the bar." His voice felt stiff and cold. "We'll all help you celebrate."

"Thank you. I didn't make the decision lightly." She took a deep breath. "It doesn't have to mean anything for you. They call it the Big Island for a reason. Not like we'll trip over each other every day. And retirement or not, your vacation can't last forever."

He was screwing this up. "Maybe I should get Harlan in here," he muttered.

"What?"

"The man can talk paint off a wall. And I

suddenly can't talk to you at all. I'm screwing this up."

Her eyebrows arched. "Then you'd better figure it out."

He stepped closer, breathing in the soft scent that was all her. It steadied him. Beat by beat, he felt his heart rate drop back to normal. This was the most important moment of the rest of his life. And, like looking at a target through a scope, everything was suddenly sharp and clear.

"I love you, Cassie. I *want* to trip over you every day and make love to you every night. If you're staying, I'm staying."

"And your friends?"

"The guys and I will sort it out. You matter most to me. Wherever you are is the place I want to call home." He cupped her cheek. "You're my North Star."

Her eyes glistened with tears. Happy tears, he hoped.

"You mean it?"

"Day and night, sweetheart, you're it. I love you." He kissed her softly, but pulled back. "Tell me you love me too."

"I do, Lane!" She boosted herself into his arms. "I love you." Holding him tightly, she kissed him.

He turned, pinning her to the wall so he could relax in the pure joy of it.

"Against my better judgment," she teased. "You're the best leap of faith ever."

"I promise you won't ever regret it," he vowed.

"Same goes." She cradled his face between her palms. "Did you hear me say my new job comes with a suite here at the resort?"

Huh. "No," he admitted. "I didn't catch that. I was a little preoccupied."

She cocked her head. "Preoccupied or panicked?"

"A man is allowed to have a few secrets."

Her hips rocked into his. "Not from his North Star."

He nuzzled her neck, making her giggle. "In that case, I admit to panic. But if you try to tell anyone, I'll deny it to my grave."

"I promise to never divulge your secrets, Lane Benning." Her hands glided over his shoulders, coming to rest over his heart. "And I promise to love you forever. In sunshine or rain, earthquakes or lava, I will always be yours."

The words felt more significant than any vows they might exchange as part of a formal ceremony. Still, he discovered he wanted that traditional moment. Wanted to see her in a wedding dress and stand with her in front of friends and family to make his promises. He wanted to celebrate their commitment, wanted to create memories and a special day just for the two of them.

But there was time. Time to find a ring and the right place to propose, and time to plan an unforgettable day. Because they'd been through hell, and there were challenges ahead for sure. But he had more confidence than ever. With Cassie at his side, they could conquer whatever life aimed their way.

"The guys are waiting," he remembered, before he let things go too far right here against the wall. "Harlan is going to give me crap. You may have to come to my defense."

She laughed. "Why would he do that?"

"Because once we tell them all of this, he'll make some bold claim about knowing the exact moment I fell in love with you."

"You did say he was the best at reading people."

"Uh huh." He opened the door for her and they walked out. "That's not for him to know. The man can't be right about everything."

"Are you sure?" She pressed the button for the elevator, then went up on her toes to give him another kiss. "You'd better tell me when it happened," she suggested. "If you don't, I might think your friend knows best."

He stepped into the elevator, and thankfully they were alone. He pulled her close and smoothed her hair back from her face. Of course he'd tell her.

"Harlan would tell you I fell in love at first sight. The moment I saw you on the beach." Had it been only a little over a week ago?

"You didn't?"

He shook his head, delighted by the sparkle in her eyes. "That was lust."

"Do go on." She wound her arms around his neck, her body pressing in close. "I can't wait to hear this."

The woman was the best kind of distraction. He had to work to remember what they were talking about. "My heart fell at your feet, irrevocably, during that conversation about funerals and closure." His hands slid up and down her back. "I'm surprised, offended even, that you didn't hear the thud."

"I probably wrote it off as an aftershock."

"We've had our share of those," he agreed. "Volcanoes, earthquakes, and a few wild goose chases. I'd say it's the perfect start for you and me."

"Perfect?"

The elevator doors opened and her laughter spilled out ahead of them. They walked through the lobby hand in hand, out into another balmy Hawaiian evening.

"You have to admit ours is an exciting love story." One he hoped to share with his grandchildren someday. "Do you want kids?"

She laughed, then jerked to a stop. "You're serious."

He'd shocked her, but he didn't believe for a

second that he'd rushed anything. She knew him, knew he was hers no matter what.

Her smile faded as she moved closer. "You want kids." It sounded more like an accusation, but her gaze had gone dreamy.

"With you, yes." An image of her carrying their child nearly brought him to his knees. "How else would we get grandkids who will sit and listen to me tell them about winning your heart?"

"Kids aren't an automatic grandkid metric." Her fingertips traced his shirt buttons. "Look at you. I guess I finally peeled away enough of your layers to find a traditional gooey center."

It surprised him too. Then again, he was only this way because of her. "Cassie."

She looked up and he didn't wait for an answer, it was shining in her eyes. "You are all the family I need," she said. "Adding children would be the sweetest bonus. Growing old with you, that's sure to be an adventure, grandkids or not."

He agreed with every fiber of his being. Not trusting his words, he kissed her soundly.

There was no way to be sure what the future held, only that she was his true north and he was hers. Together, they could find their way through anything. Overcome any challenge. Together they could be in love for all the years ahead.

Brotherhood Protectors Hawaii World
Team Koa Alpha

Lane Unleashed - Regan Black

Harlan Unleashed - Stacey Wilk

Raider Unleashed - Lori Matthews

Waylen Unleashed - Jen Talty

Kian Unleashed - Kris Norris

ABOUT THE AUTHOR

Regan Black, a USA Today and internationally bestselling author, writes award-winning, action-packed romances featuring kick-butt heroines and the sexy heroes who fall in love with them. Raised in the Midwest and California, she and her husband enjoy an empty-nest life in the South Carolina Lowcountry where the rich blend of legend, romance, and history fuels her imagination.

For book news and special offers, subscribe to Regan's newsletter.

Keep up with Regan online:
www.ReganBlack.com
Follow Regan on Amazon
Follow Regan on BookBub
Facebook Reader Group

BROTHERHOOD PROTECTORS WORLD

ORIGINAL SERIES BY ELLE JAMES

Brotherhood Protectors Hawaii World

Team Koa Alpha

Lane Unleashed - Regan Black

Harlan Unleashed - Stacey Wilk

Raider Unleashed - Lori Matthews

Waylen Unleashed - Jen Talty

Kian Unleashed - Kris Norris

Brotherhood Protectors Yellowstone World

Team Wolf

Guarding Harper - - Desiree Holt

Guarding Hannah - Delilah Devlin

Guarding Eris - Reina Torres

Guarding Payton - Jen Talty

Guarding Leah - Regan Black

Team Eagle

Booker's Mission - Kris Norris

Hunter's Mission - Kendall Talbot

Gunn's Mission - Delilah Devlin

Xavier's Mission - Lori Matthews

Wyatt's Mission - Jen Talty

Corbin's Mission - Jen Talty

Tyson's Mission - Delilah Devlin

Knox's Mission - Barb Han

Colton's Mission - Kendall Talbot

Walker's Mission - Kris Norris

Brotherhood Protectors Colorado World

Team Watchdog

Mason's Watch - Jen Talty

Asher's Watch - Leanne Tyler

Cruz's Watch - Stacey Wilk

Kent's Watch- Deanna L. Rowley

Ryder's Watch- Kris Norris

Team Raptor

Darius' Promise - Jen Talty

Simon's Promise - Leanne Tyler

Nash's Promise - Stacey Wilk

Spencer's Promise - Deanna L. Rowley

Logan's Promise - Kris Norris

Team Falco

Fighting for Esme - Jen Talty

Fighting for Charli - Leanne Tyler

Fighting for Tessa - Stacey Wilk

Fighting for Kora - Deanna L. Rowley

Fighting for Fiona - Kris Norris

Athena Project

Beck's Six - Desiree Holt

Victoria's Six - Delilah Devlin

Cygny's Six - Reina Torres

Fay's Six - Jen Talty

Melody's Six - Regan Black

Team Trojan

Defending Sophie - Desiree Holt

Defending Evangeline - Delilah Devlin

Defending Casey - Reina Torres

Defending Sparrow - Jen Talty

Defending Avery - Regan Black

BROTHERHOOD PROTECTORS

ORIGINAL SERIES BY ELLE JAMES

Remy (#1)

Gerard (#2)

Lucas (#3)

Beau (#4)

Rafael (#5)

Valentin (#6)

Landry (#7)

Simon (#8)

Maurice (#9)

Jacques (#10)

Brotherhood Protectors Yellowstone

Saving Kyla (#1)

Saving Chelsea (#2)

Saving Amanda (#3)

Saving Liliana (#4)

Saving Breely (#5)

Saving Savvie (#6)

Saving Jenna (#7)

Saving Peyton (#8)

Saving Londyn (#9)

Brotherhood Protectors Colorado

SEAL Salvation (#1)

Brotherhood Protectors

ABOUT ELLE JAMES

ELLE JAMES also writing as MYLA JACKSON is a *New York Times* and *USA Today* Bestselling author of books including cowboys, intrigues and paranormal adventures that keep her readers on the edges of their seats. When she's not at her computer, she's traveling, snow skiing, boating, or riding her ATV, dreaming up new stories. Learn more about Elle James at www.ellejames.com

Website | Facebook | Twitter | GoodReads | Newsletter | BookBub | Amazon

Or visit her alter ego Myla Jackson at mylajackson.com
Website | Facebook | Twitter | Newsletter

Follow Me!
www.ellejames.com
ellejamesauthor@gmail.com